HER OREGON TRAIL MINER

LONDON JAMES

ONE

CORA

She'd heard someone say that an orphan was an orphan for life, no matter if they found another family or not. At the time she'd heard it, and perhaps even most of her youth, Cora Randall didn't think those words made any sense. How can an orphan still feel lonely if they had another family? Wouldn't that be foolish of them?

But the older she got, the more she learned that perhaps there had been some truth to the saying. The only problem was that she just couldn't put her finger on why. Perhaps it was because deep down, although she knew another family would love her as though she were their own daughter, it still wasn't the same.

She would never be genuinely theirs.

Just like she never would truly be Winona's daughter.

She'd lived almost her whole life at the orphanage with Winona, and in that time, she'd nearly gone home with ten different families. Ten different husbands and wives in various stages of marriage, whether recently married or had been married for years and had other children at home. She never knew why none of them adopted her, but in the end, and looking back on it now, she knew each one of the couples who had walked out with a different child had made the right choice. There was no better place for her than Kensington. But even with her love for the place and Winona, there was still an emptiness inside.

She was an orphan.

She had been abandoned.

Perhaps that was what the person meant when they said an orphan was an orphan for life, no matter if they found another family or not. Perhaps that was also why she longed to make her own family as much as she did. If she made one, then maybe, just maybe, she wouldn't feel like an orphan anymore. It wouldn't matter that she didn't have parents because she would have children and become a parent.

Once she was married and had a husband, she wouldn't need a father.

And once she was a mother, she wouldn't need a mother.

It was a feeling she knew down to her bones, like a dull ache that never seemed to go away no matter how much she rested or tried not to think about it. She'd been so close to finding that forever with Dr. Evans. Or at least she'd thought she had until Lark got in the way. Of course, now she knew it was God's will for them to marry, but it still didn't mean that watching Lark and Carter exchange their vows didn't hurt.

It did.

Just as it hurt watching them run off to his wagon, bidding everyone goodnight while the rest of the wagon train settled in for dinner and celebration without them. Another added sting to her chest. She had pictured herself marrying him so many times and for that dream not to come true...

She didn't want to think about it, nor did she want to think about how those images of a husband and children just shattered like a mirror dropped on the ground. Her eyes misted with tears, but she blinked them away before they could stream down her cheeks.

"A penny for your thoughts," Harper slid up beside Cora and nudged her in the shoulder.

"They look happy." Cora motioned toward the direction that Lark and Carter disappeared.

"Yes, they do. And I'm happy for them."

"I am too." Although she struggled to say the words, she said them, and deep down, she meant them even if they stung.

"Are you sure about that?" Harper raised one eyebrow, giving Cora a sideways glance.

"Yes. I am." Cora dropped her gaze, looking down at her hands as she fidgeted with her fingers. Guilt prickled in her chest. "I know I was awful to Lark, and if she doesn't wish to forgive me, then I will understand."

"She will. You just need to give her some time."

"I suppose we shall see. But I won't pretend to not know that I was difficult. I'm just scared."

"Of what?"

"Of not finding love. Of not finding a good man to marry. I want those things so bad, Harper, that sometimes I can't breathe. I know it made me lash out and react in ways I shouldn't. She was just making me so angry when she didn't like him or appreciate him."

"I think she did. It was just in a different way."

"I know that now."

"You need to stop focusing on marriage so much."

"That's easy for you to say when it's not that important to you."

"I wouldn't say that it's not. I just have other dreams that I want more." Harper gave a slight smile and cocked her head to the side.

"Ah, yes, teaching children instead of having them."

"I want them . . . someday. But yes, I would love to be a

teacher." Harper exhaled a deep breath. "In the end, I think you'll find out you'll be fine. I don't think your life will end if it takes time to find the right man. In fact, I think it would be better to wait for that right one."

Cora's stomach twisted. She wanted to believe her friend, but she didn't know if she could. "How do you know?"

"Because I do." Harper cocked her head to the side and closed one eye as though doing so made her concentrate more. "Have you ever heard of Miguel de Cervantes?"

"No. Who is that?" Although Cora answered the other young woman, she continued to stare at Carter's wagon, watching the firelight fleck off the cream-colored bonnet with the shadows of everyone gathered around the fire, enjoying a huge feast everyone contributed to.

"He's an author from the 1600s, and he wrote a novel titled Don Quixote."

Cora rolled her eyes. "Why are you telling me this?"

"I'm telling you this because there is a phrase in the novel that I think you should hear."

"And what is that?"

"When one door is shut, another is opened."

"And what is that supposed to mean?" Cora glanced at Harper, raising one eyebrow. A slight hint of annoyance fluttered in her chest. Just what on earth was the point of this conversation?

"It means that just because you were wrong about Dr. Evans and it doesn't mean you won't find another man to love and marry. He isn't the only man on this earth. He isn't even the only man on this wagon train." Harper nudged her again and then tilted her head to motion toward another man leaning against a nearby wagon, staring at the two of the women.

Just as with the wagon bonnet, the firelight flecked off his face, illuminating parts of his cheeks and eyes while darkening the rest of him. Cora had seen the man before. He was one of the single men on the wagon train, and although she hadn't noticed him before, she did now. He was tall and slender. Not exactly the type of man she usually looked at. But there was a handsomeness about him in a way.

"Do you know his name?" she asked Harper.

"No. I don't. But I'm sure he'd happily tell you what it is. He's been staring at you all evening." Harper giggled, and the two women looked in the man's direction.

He tipped his hat.

"Why don't you go talk to him?" Harper nudged her a third time, and before Cora could agree or not, she backed away, leaving Cora standing alone as she continued to stare at the man, hoping that he would take her silent hint to approach her instead.

A hint he happily took.

"It is a nice evening for a wedding, isn't it?" he asked, moving alongside her.

"Yes, it was."

The man smiled. "I hope your sister and the doctor are happy."

"She's not my sister."

"Oh." The man blinked. "I guess I just thought . . ." He let his voice trail off as he glanced over toward Dr. Evan's wagon, where the married couple had vanished.

Cora glanced at the man, trying to ignore how her gut twisted a little. It wasn't an immediate attraction, or at least like she'd felt with Dr. Evans, but there was still the pulse of something—whatever it was.

"I'm Sam, by the way. Sam Wright." He stuck his hand out to shake hers.

"Cora Randall."

"So, are you related to any of the other women you're traveling with?" he asked, raising one eyebrow.

"No." She chewed on her lip. She hadn't ever questioned

telling a man about her past until now, and while she didn't know why she did with Sam, she listened to her stomach. She didn't need anyone judging her on top of all the other emotional turmoil the day had brought her,

"I see. I thought you were all related. Well, at least you aren't traveling alone. Of course, a woman shouldn't anyway, but still." A slight chuckle left his lips, and he cleared his throat. "Are you settling in Oregon or somewhere along the way?"

"We are heading to Oregon."

"Do you have family there waiting for you or anyone you are meeting?" He raised one eyebrow.

"Anyone, as in?"

"Oh, just anyone." Although he didn't say the word, she could guess by his tone that he wondered if she was a mail-order bride on her way to meet her future husband. Her stomach fluttered. He was interested in knowing whether or not she was betrothed.

"No. I'm not meeting anyone." She chewed on her lip again. "Do you have anyone waiting for you?"

"Nah. I'm just heading out there alone to make a different life." He glanced over his shoulder, pausing before he looked back at the camp and everyone celebrating around the campfire. His shoulders stiffened as though certain thoughts crossed his mind then he seemed to soften.

"I think that's probably what everyone is doing," she said.

"Yeah, I suppose you're right." He shoved his hands into his pockets as he rocked back and forth on his toes and heels. "So, if your family isn't in Oregon, where are they?"

"Um . . . I'm not sure. Last I heard, they were leaving Missouri. But . . . I don't speak to them anymore, so I don't know if they ended up leaving or not." While it wasn't the whole truth, it wasn't exactly a lie either. From what she'd gathered over the years from Winona, her parents gave her to the orphanage as a baby because they were headed out of the state and didn't want to take her with them. "A baby is too much work for traveling," her father had told the headmistress. Cora didn't know how many years she'd believed that to be true. Nor did she know when she figured out it wasn't, but watching the children, plus a rather heavily pregnant German woman on the wagon train, she knew that her father had been wrong.

"Oh? You don't speak to them?" he asked.

"No. I don't."

"I don't speak to my family either."

"Why?"

"They just don't understand me."

Cora inhaled a deep breath, glancing around the camp. He wasn't the most intoxicating to speak to, yet she also couldn't help but wonder if she was just as dull to him.

I should try harder, she thought.

She faced him, brushing his arm with her fingertips as she cocked her head to the side. "Have you ever heard of Miguel de Cervantes?"

His brow furrowed, and he shook his head.

"Well, he's an author—and a rather famous one, I believe—from the 1600s, and he penned a novel titled Don Quixote. In it, he wrote, 'when one door is shut, another is opened.'"

"Makes sense to me. Is this a book you've read?"

"No. I haven't read it. Of course, now I think I might like to. But I don't know if I'll ever find a copy. I wouldn't even know where to look. My friend Harper might know. She's always been into books and reading. I always thought it was just a waste of time." Cora laughed, then as the words registered in her mind, she froze. "I mean, I don't think that reading is a waste of time. I know it's important, and . . ."

"It's okay. I don't read much either, and even if I had the time, I probably wouldn't. So you won't get any complaints or judgment about your lack of reading from me."

A hint of relief spread through her chest. "At least I'm not the only one."

"I have to ask, however, if you don't read much, how do you know about the book and a quote?"

"A friend told me." She paused, looking at Sam as the firelight continued to flicker across his face. "I must admit that I think it just suits the night. Don't you think?"

"I suppose it does." He smiled. "Are you hungry?" He pointed toward the large pot of stew hanging on the fire where everyone had gathered after the wedding. Steam rose from the hot food inside.

"A little." While part of her wondered if she could eat, given her stomach was in such a knotted mess from not only watching the ceremony but in talking to Sam, she also knew if she didn't try, she would go to bed hungry. And that was something she never wanted to do. She had once a long time ago when she was a young girl and wanted to rebel against the dinner that Winona had the cooks at the orphanage serve. It had been enough of a miserable night that she never wanted to do it again.

"Shall we?" Sam asked.

She followed him toward the campfire, and then after, he motioned toward a space just for two on a log. They sat down, and after Mrs. Reed handed them each a bowl of stew, they turned toward one another.

"So, how are you liking the trail so far?" he asked.

"It's all right if you don't mind the uncomfortable wagon and long days that leave you sunburned with blisters all over your feet. Not to mention bathing in a river, a bland diet that leaves little to the imagination, and the fear of not knowing if you will live to see tomorrow."

"Yeah, I suppose it has been quite the adventure."

"Not to mention the measles outbreak. I didn't know what was going to become of everyone. It was scary."

"One of your traveling companions got sick, didn't she? The one who got married tonight to the doctor?"

"Yes. She is better now."

"I'm sure you're grateful for that."

"I am. We aren't exactly close, but I still don't wish for anything bad to happen to her."

"You aren't close?"

"No. We hardly speak unless we have to."

Sam glanced over his shoulder, then leaned in closer to Cora. Her heart skipped. "Is it true what they are saying about her?"

"Is what true?"

"That she was a woman of questionable morals. You know, a painted lady like you called her that one afternoon when you were arguing. Is it true she was a whore?"

The harshness of the word caught in Cora's throat, and her head jerked. "Um . . . I don't know if I would say it that way." She leaned away from him, slightly, uncomfortable with how his tone seemed to change.

He studied her for a second, then smiled. "You'll have to excuse me. Sometimes I forget how I'm supposed and not supposed to talk to a lady." He waved his hand as though trying to wave off his offensive language. "Still, though, that's quite the story now that I know it's true." He leaned away from her, closing one eye as though doing so helped him get a better look at Cora. "You aren't one, too, are you?"

"No." She brushed her hand against her collarbone. "I would never live that kind of life. Although, I suppose she didn't choose it. It was chosen for her. But still. I would kill myself before I even set foot in one of those places."

"Yeah." Sam's brow furrowed slightly as though different thoughts ran through his mind. Whatever they were, though, he didn't say, and Cora didn't ask. Why was it that whenever she spoke to a man, all he wanted to do was speak about Lark?

What was it with men and her? Was it her past? Were they attracted to that?

I would think they would want a proper woman, Cora thought to herself. "In the end, it doesn't matter what Lark has done or where she's been. She's married now," Cora said, hoping Sam would pick up on the words she chose. Since Lark was married, he didn't have a chance, and he needed to forget about her and not think about her.

"That's true. And as long as her husband doesn't mind . . ." Sam gave Cora a sideways glance. "I don't know if most men could handle it. Although, at the same time, I can't speak for all men, so perhaps there would be some that wouldn't be concerned and some who would."

She chewed on her lip, and her gaze moved toward him, but she didn't move her head. "I mean . . . just because Dr. Evans was fine with the notion doesn't mean that . . . say . . . you, for example, would be . . . or perhaps another man either." Yes, she was fishing for a clue into Sam's mind, and although she hoped he wouldn't catch on, a tiny part of her also wondered about him if he didn't. Surely, a fool would see right through her words.

Right?

"Are you asking me what I think about it?" he asked.

"Perhaps."

"What do you think about it?" He raised an eyebrow.

She wanted to make a face at his dismissive attempt to skirt the question, but she didn't. Why did he always seem to answer a question with a question? He glanced at her and clicked his tongue. She didn't know if his answer mattered and, if it did, how much. Would the next few words he could say make her rise to her feet and walk away? Or did it make a difference? She didn't know how she would feel if he said that he would marry a woman who worked in a brothel.

Perhaps it was only that she wanted to know more than she wanted the answer to dictate how she would feel for him.

"I don't know if I would be comfortable with a husband who thought it proper to take such a woman for his wife."

A slight smirk spread across his face. "I'm glad to hear you say that because I don't think I would be comfortable with having a woman like that as a wife."

The tension in her shoulders softened, and as she looked at him and he smiled, something tugged on her mind. He was different, but she wasn't sure if it was in a good way or not.

I just need to give him a chance, she thought. *My one door has closed now that Dr. Evans and Lark are married. Perhaps this is the other door that is opening for me. Perhaps Sam is whom God has chosen. I need to embrace it.*

TWO

CORA

"It's chilly this morning." Harper sat beside Cora, peeling slices of bacon off the chunk of meat before throwing them down on the skillet. The raw pork sizzled as it hit the hot pan and began to scrunch up as the fat turned white and began to render into a liquid. "I think this is one of the first mornings I needed my extra blanket."

Cora nodded, making a slight *ah-huh* sound.

"Did you need yours?" Harper asked.

Cora shook her head. "I stayed closer to the fire than you and Grace did, so I was fine."

"Oh. That was smart of you." Harper chuckled. "I should probably remember when we have any more cold mornings." She finished tossing a few more bacon slices on the pan and then wrapped up the rest of the meat. "So . . . are you ever going to tell me what happened last night after I left?"

"What are you two talking about?" Winona joined them near the fire, and she glanced at them both as she reached for the coffee kettle. She picked it up, poured herself a cup then set it back on the fire.

"Cora met a man last night after the wedding." Harper

tucked her chin down, and as a slight giggle weaved through her words, her cheeks flushed with a subtle pink shade.

"Oh?" Winona straightened her shoulders as she stared at Cora. Her voice held a hesitation in the tone. "And who is this young man?"

"His name is Sam Wright. He's one of the single men traveling with the wagon train."

"I think I know who he is. Is he on the taller side with blond hair?"

"And with a slightly goofy smile? Yes. That's him."

"Oh. Well, I can't say I've spoken to or heard much about him. What did you think of him? Is he nice?"

"He is." Cora paused, hesitating about the truth sitting on the tip of her tongue.

"It feels like there is a but in there." Harper flipped the bacon as she glanced from Winona to Cora.

"No. There isn't a but. Well, maybe. I don't know. There's something different about him, and I have yet to put my finger on whether or not it's a good difference."

"What do you mean?"

"I don't know. There just wasn't that initial attraction as I had with Dr. Evans."

Harper snorted. "How can anyone not have an initial attraction to Lark's new husband? Don't think you were the only one who noticed him. Lark is a lucky woman."

"Not all men will be handsome in your eyes, and that's acceptable. It's the quality of his character that matters." Winona shot Harper a slight glare, and Harper chuckled, tucking her chin to her chest.

Before she could say another word, Grace came around from the other side of the wagon, fixing a pin in her hair. "Did anyone else need an extra blanket last night?" she asked.

The three women looked at her, and she froze. "What are you talking about?"

"How not all men look like Dr. Evans." Harper laughed at her answer and then laughed even harder as Winona reached out and tried to slap at her arm.

"Oh. I agree. Lark is a lucky woman." Grace trotted over to the fire and sat down next to Harper. "Do you know who else is handsome?"

"Who?"

"Mr. Campbell, the blacksmith. Oh, and Mr. Scott, the miner from the Klondike. Although, both of them seem to keep to themselves mostly. I don't think I've ever seen either of them talk to anyone."

"I know who the blacksmith is, but who is Mr. Scott?" Cora asked the two women.

"He's the tall, dark-haired man who is always panning for gold in the river when we camp. He doesn't say much to anyone, but I've seen him a few times while getting water. I tried smiling at him, but he either didn't notice or ignored me."

"I'm sure he just didn't notice. No man would ignore you." Harper nudged her friend on the shoulder, and Grace smiled. "Anyway, he's probably just focused on finding gold which never leaves room in their minds for anything else."

"That is true." Winona took a sip of her coffee and then turned to Cora. "So, do you not like Mr. Wright, then?"

"No, I do. I just . . . I thought there would be more sparks. I suppose those can grow, though. Right?"

"Yes, they can."

"And I do wish to be married and have a family." Cora replayed most of last night in her mind. Sam was kind, and he made her smile. Two qualities that she always told herself she wanted. Surely, he wasn't the striking man she first noticed and who was now married to someone else. But what did that matter anyway? Looks weren't everything, and that point was proven when the handsome man looked past her and desired someone else instead—someone who wasn't a proper lady. She didn't want to begrudge him for his choice, but at the same time, it was all she could do. How could anyone choose a woman with that kind of a past over another woman who hadn't shared her bed with who knows how many men?

No, she thought to herself. *Don't judge. It's not your place. Just stop.*

She shook her head. "I think perhaps I will visit with him this afternoon."

"I think that sounds like a lovely idea." Winona stood, and after dumping the last bit of her coffee onto the ground, she fetched the plates, handing one to each of the women and keeping one for herself.

They served themselves breakfast, and while the three women around her began eating, Cora glanced over toward the wagon next to them. She had purposely not looked in that direction all morning, and while she wanted to resist the urge now, she didn't. While she hadn't lied about being happy for Lark and Carter last night, the thought of still seeing them together caused her stomach to flutter.

It wouldn't just be seeing them talk to one another, either.

What if she spied them sharing a kiss?

She closed her eyes, and by the time she opened them, Carter had jumped down from the back of the wagon and headed toward the campfire that had nearly died out while he and his new bride slept. He bent down, tossing a few chunks of wood and dried leaves he'd collected onto the tiny flames, and within a few minutes, the campfire had reignited. With the fire going again, he called to Lark, who stepped out of the back of the wagon wrapped in a blanket. Her long, blonde hair flowed down her back, and the strands were wavy from being tucked in a tight bun. She had the glow of a new bride and a young woman who now stood on the precipice of a new life and adventure.

And it was the kind of life and adventure that Cora longed to have for herself, and as she watched the two of them share a conversation she couldn't hear while they made breakfast together, her stomach twisted. Tears misted her eyes, and she set her plate of food down without even taking a bite.

"Is everything all right?" Winona asked.

"Yes, of course." Cora brushed her fingertips across her forehead. "I think I will bathe in the river and wash my hair. I want it to look nice and pretty for when I visit with Mr. Wright this afternoon."

"Do you want me or one of the others to go with you?" Winona asked.

"Nah, that's not necessary. It won't take long, and I could use the time alone." She glanced at her headmistress, knowing the look on Winona's face. The woman always had the same one when she questioned whether or not Cora, any of the other women, or any of the other children at the orphanage was lying to her.

How was it that she always knew?

"I'm quite nervous," Cora said, hoping the last sentence would ease Winona's suspicion.

∽

WINONA

Winona watched Cora walk away from the campfire. She didn't want to think that perhaps the young woman was lying, but something in her gut told her she was. Surely, she couldn't have fallen in love with the doctor now married to Lark, as they hadn't spent time alone or spoken to one another. Still, Winona knew Cora had feelings for the man, and to suddenly have it all ripped away by him getting married...

Perhaps that was the main reason for it all, too. It wasn't just the man that Cora was interested in—although he was a big part of the whole thing—but it was also being married.

"It's probably for the best she bathes. I could smell her from across the campfire," Harper laughed, taking the last bite of bacon. Grace's head whipped around, and her mouth fell open.

"That was mean."

"It's true. And I'm sure the same could be said about me too."

"Perhaps you should all go to the river then," Winona said, exhaling a deep breath. "But do give her some time alone. I'm afraid she needs it." Winona glanced off in the direction that Cora vanished, and an uncomfortable notion twisted in her stomach. She knew nothing of the young man Cora had spoken with last night, and while she didn't know Dr. Evans either, there was something off about the whole thing.

Perhaps Mr. Mills knows something about him, she thought.

She set the plate down and rose to her feet, pointing toward the mess they had all made cooking breakfast. "Clean this up, please," she said.

"Where are you going?" Harper asked.

"I need to have a word with Mr. Mills."

"About what?"

"That's not for you to concern yourself with. When you finish cleaning up, you may go to the river to bathe if you wish. Just try to give Cora some space."

"We will, Winona." Grace finished off the last of her breakfast and handed Harper the plate. "You wash and I'll dry?"

Winona continued to listen to them until she couldn't hear them anymore, and as she made her way over to the wagon master's wagon, a slight smile spread across her face. While Cora had made it known when certain men had caught her eye, Harper and Grace had taken a more silent approach to the matter, and hearing them speak of good-looking men that they'd noticed had surprised the headmistress. Of course, it was a good surprise, but it was a surprise, nonetheless.

Winona found Mr. Mills sitting by his campfire, tending to his morning breakfast as she approached, and as he noticed her, he stood and tipped his hat.

"Good morning, Miss Callahan," he said.

"Good morning, Mr. Mills."

He pointed toward a log he'd been sitting on. "May I offer you a seat?"

He must be in a good mood this morning, she thought. "Yes. Thank you."

"Are you hungry?" he asked, sitting beside her and pointing toward the empty hot pan on the fire.

"No. I ate already."

He nodded, then returned to cooking his morning meal by tossing chunks of bacon into a hot pan. He watched it sizzle, then stood, looking out over the horizon as the sun started peering over the trees, shining its bright light onto the camp. "It's a beautiful morning," he said.

"Yes. It is."

"It's a nice camp, too. I don't want to leave, but we need to get back on the trail."

"Are we leaving today?"

"Nah. I think another day of rest would be good. But I plan to let everyone know we will leave at dawn tomorrow morning."

"I'll be sure to get everything packed up tonight, then."

A slight grunt whispered from his lips as though he approved of her choice, and he continued cooking his breakfast, cutting up a couple of potatoes and throwing the chunks in with the sizzling meat. Winona didn't know what was more uncomfortable, the silent moments between them or the small talk that didn't hold any substance.

"Is there a reason for your visit this morning, Miss Callahan?" he finally said, pushing the meat and potatoes around in the skillet. Steam rose from the heat.

Apparently, he, too, didn't care for the awkwardness.

"Well, I have a few questions to ask you."

"All right."

"They are about someone on the wagon train."

He stopped stirring and glanced at her with one eyebrow cocked. "I beg your pardon?"

She wasn't sure if she should weave her way through the conversation more delicately or just jump into the water feet first, but as she opened her mouth, her mind decided on the latter.

"Apparently, one of the single men has taken an interest in one of the young ladies traveling with me. And I was wondering if you knew anything about him."

"Didn't you just marry off one of them?"

"Yes. But I don't see how that makes any difference."

"You didn't come to me asking about Dr. Evans."

"I know I didn't. But the circumstances were a little different. Two of the young women had met him the morning we left, and I introduced myself that first night. He was keener on the idea of meeting me, whereas I have never met Mr. Wright, and he's never made any effort to introduce himself. I don't know what it is. There's just something different about it."

"And what is it you wish to know from me?"

"Just what you know of him."

"I know he's trying to get to Oregon."

"And?"

"And he . . . paid me to get him there." Mr. Mills glanced at her with his eyebrow still raised. "I'm unsure what information you seek or why it matters."

"I just wish to know a little about him."

"So . . . ask him."

"Oh, believe me, I plan to. I just wondered if you knew anything."

"It's not my business to ask anyone about their lives, Miss Callahan."

"I know. I suppose it was foolish for me to come over here. I just thought perhaps you might have an opinion on the man, and you could offer some insight."

"Well, my opinion is that I'm rather indifferent to the man, just as I am with everyone on the wagon train. I don't make friends, Miss Callahan, if that is what you think. All of these people, yourself included, are a business transaction. Nothing more."

She stared at him for a moment, blinking as though doing so would help her deal with the utter shock she felt. She'd always suspected the man was cold, perhaps even heartless, but she wanted to believe that there was still a slight chance that perhaps somewhere deep down inside him was a warmth that just needed to be uncovered. She pictured him as she pictured an onion—with many layers that she could remove to get to the center.

"A business transaction?" She blinked even more.

"Why would it be anything more?"

"Oh, I don't know, perhaps because you spend months with these people. How can you not become friends?"

"Because I don't need friends. I need my horse and the trail. They are my friends."

"But what about basic human interaction?"

"It's been my finding, ma'am, that human interaction only leads to stress, frustration, or heartbreak."

"You can't be that cynical. Not after witnessing a wedding last night." A slight chuckle left her lips. "Lark and Carter don't share any of those things. They are in love."

"Cynical? There's nothing cynical about it. It's just the truth. When you get to my age and have led the life I have, serving in a war that took all humanity out of everything, you see beyond living your life with your head stuck in the clouds, hoping and dreaming, and wishing for love and happiness to fill your cup until your last day. But that's not real. I don't need anyone to live how I want."

"I agree that I haven't seen what you have, but I have seen stuff you probably haven't too. Children who had no hope of finding a family until one day, the perfect parents walk in the door and change that child's life forever. Even Lark, with her past . . . I suppose I just don't think the way you do."

"Oh, really? So, how many of these people will you stay in touch with after we arrive in Oregon?"

"I wasn't saying I was out to make life-long friendships. But we will be spending months together, and we are supposed to help and keep each other safe. Or are we not?"

"You are."

"So, wouldn't that require some sort of friendship?"

"Perhaps that is the case for you, Miss Callahan. But for me . . . that's my job. I've been paid to see you safely to Oregon. Period. What you do with your life and how you live it is none of my business. Just like Mr. Wright is none of my business."

Although Winona could see a side to Mr. Mills' point, there was another side, and that was where she stood. People were—as they should be—more than just a business transaction to one another, and the fact that this old man thought what he did . . .

She just couldn't find the words.

"I'm sorry that you feel such a way." She stood, brushing any dirt from the log off the back of her skirt before striding a few steps.

"Your reaction only proves my point," he called after her.

She turned, resting her hand on her hip. "And how is that, Mr. Mills?"

He smiled at her, lifting his hand and holding up three fingers. "Human interaction only leads to stress, frustration, or heartbreak." He closed one finger on his hand with each element to his list.

"Maybe in your world that is true, but not in mine. Well, except when it comes to the likes of you. I suppose, then, it is true for me, too, since you've brought me nothing but stress and frustration."

"Just as long as it's not heartbreak, I can live with that."

"Oh, that's not something you have to worry about, Mr. Mills. You would be the last man on this earth I would ever have romantic feelings for."

THREE

JASPER

Jasper Scott turned the pan over, letting the bacon grease drip onto the grass near his feet. He probably should have kept it, but he had nothing to store it in, nor had the need for it—at least not now. There would be plenty more in the coming mornings since the pork was the only meat he'd purchased in Fort Kearney not too long ago.

And he was growing tired of it.

Never again would he listen to his stomach when choosing what food supplies to buy. Ever.

For the love of Pete, I have to be smarter about this, he thought, watching the last bit of grease drip from the pan. The last thing he needed to do was prove his brothers right, even if they weren't here to see it. They'd spent he didn't know how many months before him leaving, telling him he was nothing but a fool for making such plans.

There were times he thought perhaps they were right. What kind of man leaves the life where he had a home and employment for the unknown life out West? Growing up, he never lacked for anything. His parents always provided everything he and his brothers needed. They raised their own farm animals, and he not only had all the food he could ask for, but his mother always made sure he had clothes on his back, books to read, and had even secured him a dance at the Spring Festival with Emmaline Harrison—one of the prettiest young ladies in Dyer County, Tennessee. Dozens and dozens of men had been vying for a spot on her dance card; and out of them all, he was one of the lucky ten or so.

"Once you spin her around that floor," his mama had told him, "she will be putty in your hands. She won't even want to look at another man."

Unfortunately, he hadn't stuck around to find out if Mama would have been right or not. Instead, he packed up everything he could fit into a wagon and headed to Independence to head out on the next wagon train to Oregon. Sometimes he could kick himself for leaving Emmaline without a spot filled, but he was sure another man stepped up to take his place just fine.

I wonder if she married any of them, he thought. *Surely, she was at least courting someone by now.*

Of course, he had once hoped to marry someone like Emmaline—if not the lovely woman herself. But he also couldn't deny that part of his desire came from Mama. Even though he had two older brothers, it was always him that she bugged for the pitter-patter of little feet of grandchildren. Perhaps it was because she knew Thomas was too busy with his schooling and Justin was too busy having too much fun in all the places he shouldn't be in.

Jasper had always heard that middle children were always the defiant ones in the family, and Justin Scott was no exception. He was about as fond of love, marriage, and children as Mama was of mice in the kitchen. Poor mice never stood a chance with that woman and her rolling pin.

Of course, Jasper didn't know how he felt about those things either. Sure, he supposed he would find himself a lovely young lady and settle down one day. But right now, that wasn't on his mind. Even if a few pretty women were on this wagon train, he couldn't help but notice. Still, even if he would get a little lost in watching them laugh or smile, he knew he had other dreams he wanted to accomplish first.

One of them was finding gold in the California hills.

No one in his family had understood his need to go. Not that he needed them too, but he could have done without the snickers behind his back. He thought of the morning he left and how Mama sobbed, and Pa asked him if he was sure he wanted to leave his job on the farm. It wasn't that he wanted to. It was that he needed to, and while Pa didn't say much after Jasper answered his question, Jasper could have sworn that deep down, Pa at least saw his side—even if he didn't fully get it.

"I'll be right back." A voice caught Jasper's attention, and he glanced over as the Doctor and his new wife rounded their wagon. The doctor kissed his wife on the lips and then on the forehead before he grabbed the doctor's bag from the back of the wagon and headed across the camp. His wife took to tending clothes that needed folding from a basket, and although she never looked at Jasper directly, he could tell she knew he was watching her by the subtle way she could angle her jaw to help her look at him out the corner of her eye.

Jasper cleared his throat and looked the other way, kneeling in the grass near the bucket of sudsy water he'd used to wash his plate, fork, and knife after breakfast. He dunked the pan in and then used a rag to wash the burned bits of meat that had stuck to the pan and the last bit of grease from the cast iron.

The last thing he wanted to do was stare at the poor woman, and that's what he'd done.

Just perfect, Jasper, he thought. *Angering the doctor's wife and possibly the doctor himself if she tells him you were staring at her is about the dumbest thing you could do.*

"Good morning," another voice said, coming from her direction. So deep in tone Jasper hadn't heard it before, and he fought the urge to ignore it and not look in the direction of the doctor's wife again.

"My husband isn't here, Mister. He's visiting the German couple. You can find him over at their wagon," the wife said.

What was her name again, he wondered. *I heard it at the wedding last night. Lark? Was that it? I think it was.*

Jasper chewed on his lip. It was never right to listen in on another's conversations, or at least that is what Mama always told him when she caught him sitting at the top of the stairs listening to her and Pa's nightly chats about the farm or whether or not Mr. Dixon did or didn't pay her enough for the eggs she took to the general store that morning.

"I'm sorry, Sir—"

"It's Mr. Wright." The man's voice had a slight more bite to it which caught Jasper's ear.

"I'm sorry, Mr. Wright, but I can't help you. I'm not a doctor or a nurse. My husband is, and he's not here, so perhaps it would be better if you come back later."

"I don't want to come back later."

Jasper glanced over as the man inched closer to Mrs. Evans.

"Perhaps I could just wait here." His voice changed, and a slight seductive hint whispered through his words.

Jasper couldn't help himself any longer, and he looked in their direction just as the man moved closer to Mrs. Evans. She took a step back, and her shoulders stiffened.

"I don't think that is a good idea," she said.

"Why? Do you think I'm going to bite you or something?" He chuckled as though trying to laugh at a joke. "Wait. Are you into that type of thing?" He moved closer.

"You need to leave." Although her tone was defiant, and Jasper could tell she wanted to stand her ground, she took another step back, running into the side of the wagon. Her body bounced slightly off the wood, and she reached behind her, wrapping her fingers around the nearest wagon wheel.

"Oh, come on. I know about your past and what you are."

"I don't know what you're talking about." Her brow furrowed.

"You used to work in a brothel." He reached up and brushed the back of his index finger along her temple. "You're a . . . what is a way I can say it . . . painted lady. You'll share a bed with any man who walks into the room."

"I never worked there as a whore, if that's what you are saying." Her voice growled, and she leaned forward for a moment as though doing so would emphasize the anger that pulsed through her veins at Mr. Wright's assumption.

He snorted. "Your husband isn't around. You don't have to lie."

"I'm not lying." She recoiled from him and clenched her jaw. "Please leave." Her words hissed through her teeth.

"I bet you were the most popular one at the place." He reached up to stroke her face once more, and she jerked away from him.

"I said, leave!"

Jasper couldn't take another minute, and he stood, turning toward the two of them. "Is everything all right, Mrs. Evans," he said.

Both of them whipped their heads toward him, and while Mrs. Evans closed her eyes as though relief had just washed through her shoulders, the man glared back at Jasper. He clenched his hand in a fist and slacked his jaw to one side.

"This is none of your business," the man said to him.

"Oh, but I think that it is. Especially when Dr. Evans isn't around." Jasper took a few steps toward them and pointed toward Mr. Wright. "I believe Mrs. Evans told you to leave, twice in fact, so I think it's time for you to leave. If you need to see the doctor, I will tell him to come find you after he returns."

"Or I can stay and wait for him."

Mrs. Evans glanced between the two men and stepped another few steps away from Mr. Wright.

"I don't think she wants you to wait, and after hearing her tell you to leave, I'm going to have to inform you that either you do what she says, or else I will escort her to her husband and not only tell him about what has happened here but will also inform the wagon master."

Jasper never liked being the type to go to someone else, tattling on another's behavior, especially when he was more than capable—and willing—to handle the problem on his own. But in this instance, he felt that even if he pummeled Mr. Wright into the ground, the man wouldn't take no for an answer unless that no came from not only Dr. Evans but the wagon master himself.

"I'm pretty sure Mr. Mills won't take too kindly knowing you've been bothering this woman."

Mr. Wright furrowed his brow and held his hands up. "Fine. I'll leave."

"I'll let the doctor know you're looking for him when he returns."

"Don't bother." Mr. Wright backed away, shaking his head. "I didn't need anything from him anyway."

Without another word, Mr. Wright left, and as he vanished around the wagon, Mrs. Evans clutched her chest and took several breaths.

"Are you all right?" Jasper asked her.

She dropped her gaze to the ground and nodded but didn't say anything.

"You're welcome to wait for your husband at my wagon. I will leave you alone."

"No." She shook her head, then lifted her face to the sky, blinking as though she was fighting back tears. "I can either go find him, or I will visit my friends."

"Are you sure?"

"Yes. I don't need your help." A slight growl left her lips, and she closed her eyes for a second before slapping her hand across her forehead. She bit her lip and then turned toward him. "I'm sorry. I didn't mean to be rude. Thank you for intervening when you did."

"You're welcome. And I'm sorry if I overstepped."

"You didn't."

"Do you want me to keep a watch out in case he returns?"

"No, you don't have to."

Although there was part of him who wanted to argue, he also saw the look in her eyes, and it told him that no matter how rattled she felt, she wanted to be left alone. He motioned toward the basket of laundry. "I'll let you get back to your chores then. It was nice . . . meeting you, Mrs. Evans."

"You too. Mister?"

"Jasper Scott."

"Mr. Scott, it was nice meeting you, too."

Before he could say another word, Mrs. Evans spun and trotted off toward another wagon. Watching her leave, a hint of pity whispered through his chest. He felt terrible for the woman; not only had her past been the subject of many conversations around the camp—none of which Jasper had ever engaged in—but now this man thought he could approach her, even knowing she was now married. Well, not all men. He certainly, never had that thought, and he doubted the other husbands would either. But Mr. Wright hadn't hesitated.

Jasper bent down and fetched the bucket of sudsy water, and after dumping it, he put everything away in the wagon and grabbed his gold pan. Perhaps if he was lucky, he could stay out of anything that might happen due to Mr. Wright's actions and find some gold in the process. If he found enough, he could buy more supplies at the next fort the wagon train passed through.

And I won't buy pork, no matter how cheap it might be.

FOUR

CORA

Water dripped from Cora's hair as she fastened the last button on her blouse. Her clothes were slightly damp from her dressing before her skin thoroughly dried, and they stuck to her in a few places, tightening around her as she moved. It was like a hug, yet it was also an annoying one. She loathed wet clothes—even the ones just moistened with enough water to make them stick.

She sat down on the sandy beach along the river and groaned as she tried—and failed—to wipe the grains of sand from her feet.

"Just another enjoyment from trail life," she whispered to herself as a slight groan left her lips.

The grass behind her moved, and as she spun to face the sound, a man appeared, stopping dead in his tracks. She'd seen him around before but didn't know his name, and she couldn't remember if he was the miner or the blacksmith that Harper and Grace were talking about this morning.

"Oh. I'm sorry. I didn't know anyone was here." He turned to leave, but she called out to him.

"It's all right. I was just about finished."

He turned back and pointed toward the river. "Do you mind?"

"To share it? Not at all. The river is yours."

He smiled, chuckling a little. "Well, technically, it belongs to the United States government, but I think I'll take it for now."

Was that supposed to be a joke, she wondered as she watched him continue through the grass and out onto the sandy beach. He had an oddly shaped round pan tucked under one arm. *Ah, then that makes him the miner. What was his name again? Was he Mr. Scott or Mr. Campbell?*

She knew they had talked about both of the men but had forgotten which one of them was described as taller and which one was shorter and stout.

"I'm Jasper Scott, by the way." He nodded toward her.

He's the miner.

"Cora Randall." She gave a slight wave and then continued to wipe at the sand on her feet. Instead of wiping it off, it spread over her skin, and some even transferred to her hands. She glanced up at the sky, rolling her eyes.

"It's nice to meet you." He nodded again, then turned his attention toward the river, kneeling at the water's edge. "Do you have a bucket?"

"I beg your pardon?"

"Do you have a bucket?"

"No. Why? Do you need one?"

"If I fill a bucket with water, I can pour it over my feet to get all the sand off."

"I already have slightly wet clothes. I don't want wet stockings and shoes."

"Yeah, I don't either. That's why I let them dry in the sun first. It takes a bit, but at least I don't have to deal with sand being in my shoes. I think that is worse than being wet."

"Well, that's true. But I don't have a bucket."

"I can help you, then." He dunked the pan into the water,

scooping until it was full before he rose to his feet, made his way over to her, and poured the water onto her toes. The sand washed away in seconds. "There. Is that good enough, or do you want more?"

"No, that's fine. I appreciate your help."

"No problem. If you set them on your boots, then they won't get dirty again while they dry." A smile inched across his face, and her stomach fluttered. Harper hadn't been wrong in saying that the miner was handsome. "Or I suppose I should say you're welcome. That's the more proper thing to say. Right? I think that's what my mama always used to say." He chuckled again.

"I don't know. But I think they both could work."

"Fair enough." He made his way back over to the water and knelt as he looked over the horizon. "It's going to be a beautiful day."

Although he said it aloud, Cora got the impression it was more noted for his own gain and not something he was either saying to her or looking for a response from her and the way he seemed to take in the sight of the landscape around them made her almost want to soak it all in just the same. She suddenly felt as though she'd taken it all for granted, not appreciating the beauty of it all because she was so focused on the hardships.

She glanced down at her feet, noticing how the sun had already begun to dry them. Her shoes weren't the most comfortable footrests, but at least they were keeping the sand at bay.

"I'll have to remember the bucket trick next time," she said, breaking the silence between them. "I don't know why I didn't think about it before."

He shrugged. "It's hard to think about everything we need out here. Not to mention, if we knew everything up front, I think life would get boring. There's joy in learning something new every day. It's also humbling."

"I've never once heard anyone say their ignorance is humbling."

He glanced at her. "I'm not sure ignorance is the right word. It's rather strong, don't you think?"

"It means not knowing, does it not?"

"Well, yeah, it does."

"And you just said learning something new every day is humbling. And if you're learning about something, then you were ignorant to it beforehand."

"Well, technically."

"What do you mean technically?"

"For the most part, I've always been told ignorance is a bad thing. By definition, ignorance means lacking knowledge or awareness in general and being uneducated or unsophisticated. So, by that meaning, one could take it that the ignorant are uneducated and unsophisticated. I may have grown up on a farm in the middle of Tennessee, but I'd like to think of myself as educated and sophisticated." He straightened his shoulders and lifted his chin as though he thought taking the stance of a stiff gentleman would help his claim. "Ignorant can also mean discourteous or rude—two things that I strive not to ever be."

She stared at him for a moment, then laughed. "What on earth are we even talking about?" she asked as she settled.

He laughed too. "I have no idea."

"I have to have conversations like that with Harper, and even then, it's exhausting. I don't wish to have more."

"Harper?"

"Miss McCall. Another woman traveling in my wagon party."

"Ah, yes. Of course. Wait. Does that mean y'all aren't sisters?" His brow furrowed, and he lifted his hand, swirling one finger in the air as if there were more people around them, and that was the y'all he was talking about.

"No. We aren't."

"And the woman you're traveling with, the older one?"

"She is my headmistress."

"Like for schooling? Like a teacher?"

Cora fought a chuckle at the way he spoke. She'd only heard a southern accent a few times in her life, and she'd always loved it. She didn't know why. There was just something about it that always made her smile and brought a flush of warmth to her cheeks. "You could say she's something like that. She was the headmistress at the orphanage where I was living."

"An orphanage?"

She cocked her head to the side, biting her lip for a moment as questions about the man fired off in her mind. "Where are you from?" she asked, more interested in the answer than trying to distract him from asking about her past.

"A little town called Bell Buckle in Tennessee. It's in Bedford County. What about you?"

"Independence, Missouri."

"How long were you living at the orphanage?"

"I was just a baby when my parents left me on the doorstep one night."

"Wow. That's . . . well, I'm sorry that happened to you." He glanced down at his lap and adjusted his knees in the sand. "I couldn't imagine not knowing my ma and pa." He blinked and shook his head, and as he paused as though he was continuing to think about a future without his parents, she cocked her head to the side, trying to picture his family in her mind. Did they look the same as him, only slightly older and perhaps with a little gray in their hair and wrinkles around their eyes? And speaking of hair, was it chocolate like his, and what color of eyes did they have? She didn't know why she wondered such things about a stranger. Perhaps it was because she didn't know what her own parents looked like, and she always wondered if she looked like them—and how much—or not.

"Do you have any brothers or sisters?" she asked.

"Two brothers. They are both older than me."

"Did they stay in Bell Buckle? Or did they leave too?"

"They stayed. Ma and Pa own a big ranch, one of the biggest in Belford County, and they needed the help. They were sure mad at me when I decided to leave."

"Mad at you? Why?"

"Because now they have to do their chores and split mine." He chuckled. "I don't care what they think, though. I'm headed to California for me and not for anyone else."

"So, you're not going to Oregon?"

"Nah. I will head south as soon as we make it to Fort Hall. Hopefully, I can find another wagon train to travel with, but if I don't, I'll go alone."

"Isn't that dangerous?"

"I suppose it is. But I don't want to go to Oregon, so I will risk it."

Cora watched the young man for a moment, thinking about whether or not she thought he was brave or stupid for going off alone. Of course, there could be arguments on both sides of the coin, and while some would say he was smart, others would say he's a fool. She wasn't sure which one she would have to agree with.

Jasper turned away from her, glancing down at his pan before grabbing it and dunking it into the water.

"Are you panning for gold?" she asked.

"Yeah . . . well . . . I'm trying. I'm not sure if I'm doing a good job of it." He chuckled, then scooped up a bit of silt and sand from the bottom of the river.

"So what do you do exactly?"

"Well, from what I learned—which I'm not sure about the old man who taught me—but you start with collecting sand and rocks. Then, the basic idea is to swirl the pan so that the heaviest stuff stays on the bottom and the lightest stays on top."

"Like floats? I didn't think rocks float."

"Nah, they don't, but it's not about them floating. It's just that you can tell what is heavy and what is light. Do you want to watch?" He motioned toward the pan and smiled.

A flutter whispered through her stomach and she nodded, slipping on her stockings and shoes and not caring to tie the laces before she moved over to Jasper and knelt in the sand beside him.

"I go back and forth thinking that it's the easiest thing in the world to the hardest," he said.

"Why?"

"Because you have to be careful when swirling it and make sure you don't lose anything out of the pan when moving it around. If you aren't careful, you will lose gold."

"Wouldn't you be able to see it?"

"Not necessarily. Gold flakes—and even nuggets—can be small, and if you aren't paying attention, you could miss them."

"I didn't know they could be small. I thought they would be big."

"Well, I mean, I would love to find all the big ones." He chuckled again, swirling the pan. "But I haven't had that kind of luck."

"Have you found a lot of gold?"

"Not yet. I have a little that I've found here and there, but there's not much out here. Not like they've been finding in California. I've got big plans to find a claim and make as much money as I can." He swirled the pan a few more times, then tipped it, pushing the rocks around.

"What about a wife and family?"

He scrunched his face. "I ain't got no time for all that mess right now. But in a few years . . . I guess I'll make room for it. It was fun seeing the wedding the other night. That was the first one I'd been to in a long time. Isn't the young woman who got married traveling with your party? Or I suppose was traveling with your party?"

"Yes. She is one of the girls from the orphanage too."

"I bet you're happy for her then. They seem happy with her and the doctor." Jasper smiled as though he was picturing the new husband and wife in his mind. Then he snorted and shook his head. "Nope. No time for that right now," he muttered to himself.

Cora chewed on her thumbnail as he continued to swirl the pan around. His words weren't exactly what she wanted to hear from him, even if it was foolish to think about it or be disappointed. Of course, she wasn't courting Sam Wright, but the other night had meant something, at least to her.

She cleared her throat. "Is there anything in here?" she asked, trying to distract herself. She couldn't help but feel slightly excited, and she didn't know why. What did it matter if this man found any gold? It meant nothing to her.

"I don't think so." He continued to swirl it for a bit, then rechecked it before repeating the whole process twice before dumping it all back into the river. He groaned. "I was hoping to find something, but either I'm not looking in the right spot, or there's nothing here." He looked in one direction and then the other, studying the river. His brow furrowed.

"Are you going to keep trying?" she asked.

"I don't know. I think I might head down river a ways. You can come if you like."

She bit her lip. Part of her wanted to go, but the other part knew she had planned to visit Sam this afternoon, and she didn't want to leave him waiting for her.

"I'm sorry, but I can't. I have someone I'm visiting with this afternoon, and . . . well, I can't."

"All right. You have a nice day, Miss Randall."

"You too."

She watched him pack up his belongings, and with one last nod toward her, he made his way down the river, weaving through the thick grass until he vanished behind some trees.

Part of her wished she could toss out the proper thing to do and go with him, but the fact that he was determined to head to California and not to Oregon stopped her.

Not to mention, he wasn't looking to get married either.

I'm not waiting any longer than I have to, she thought. *I will get married before we reach the next fort.*

FIVE

CORA

By the time Cora finished her hair and headed toward Sam's wagon, she had worked herself into a rather anxious lather. Thoughts of Sam and thoughts of Jasper had collided with one another, and while she knew deep down Jasper wasn't what she wanted, there was a difference to him. Something she couldn't put her finger on.

"It doesn't matter," she said to herself. "You've chosen Sam." She shook her head and pretended to brush her shoulders as though she thought the action would vanquish the thoughts from her mind—even if it didn't seem to help.

Throughout the early morning, the other travelers had eaten breakfast, cleaned up their camps, and were already moving about, either packing or getting ready for the next leg of the trip. Winona had mentioned last night after the wedding that she'd heard the word around camp that Mr. Mills had wanted to leave in the morning now that they were a few weeks behind schedule.

Cora's heart thumped a bit harder as she neared Sam's wagon, and her fingers trembled as she reached up and felt around the back of her hair, checking to ensure the strands were still tucked in her tight bun. She didn't know what she would say to him or what they would talk about, but she hoped it wouldn't matter as soon as she saw him.

She hoped they could pick up where they left off after the wedding.

"Mr. Wright?" she called out as she neared the wagon. "Are you here?"

No one responded, and she looked around the camp, staring at the firepit for a moment as she noticed the smoke and steam rising from the charred piece of wood in the middle. The fire had been put out not that long ago. Perhaps even just minutes before she arrived.

He had been here.

Or at least he had been not too long ago.

She rounded the wagon, lifting her hand to her face to shield the afternoon sun as she looked around the camp. Movement caught her attention, and as she looked off into the distance, she spied Sam walking toward the trees surrounding the camp.

She bit her lip. "Should I follow," she asked herself. "Or should I wait for him to return?"

The pull for each choice tugged at her. On the one hand, she didn't want to bother him if he was headed off to do something that was none of her business. But on the other hand, she didn't want to sit around his camp, twiddling her thumbs while she waited. She didn't know how long he would be or when he would return. She thought of returning to her wagon, but the idea of facing Harper, Grace, and even Winona with the questions they would surely ask her made her feel like rocks in her stomach.

No, she thought, *I can't go back. Not now.*

She bit her lip again and clicked her tongue, thinking about what Winona would tell her to do in this situation. Surely, the proper thing to do would be to sit down and wait, which would be her headmistress's choice of action—or so she thinks—but did she wish to do it?

Wasn't it . . . what was the saying again. . . 'the time is of the essence'?

Especially now?

Not to mention, with Sam being so keen on her, surely he wouldn't mind her going after him. In fact, he might even think it was a good thing. She glanced up at the sky, whispering a slight prayer as she trotted toward the trees, entering the thick brush where she last saw him.

Leaves crunched under her feet as she made her way deeper into the heart of the brush. The trees towered above her, like sentinels of nature, while the crisp spring afternoon air was alive with the sound of birds chirping to one another while fluttering from branch to branch. Their chirped melodies weaved through the rustling of leaves underfoot until she rounded a large bush and heard several loud grunts.

She spun to the left, seeing Sam chopping viciously at a tree with an axe. His face was contorted with a rage she hadn't seen before, nor thought he was capable of. Sweat poured down his forehead as he swung the axe with all his might several times, each blow ringing out in the otherwise silent forest. She flinched every time the steel blade dug into the bark. The tree shook under Sam's relentless assault, bark flew in all directions, and with his actions a display of unbridled frustration and fury, he had no idea that she watched from a distance.

She stood there momentarily; her mind was racing with thoughts of what she should do. Should she stay? Should she flee? It was obvious that something had the man riled up, but she still didn't know if she wanted to know what it was or not. He swung the axe several more times, and the sharp blade bit into the tree trunk. She could feel the anger radiating off him, and it churned in her stomach.

Eventually, exhausted and spent, Sam turned as though he

knew she was watching him. His brow furrowed, and he dropped the axe. The tool made of steel and wood fell to the ground with a loud thump that made Cora flinch just as much as she had every time he had pounded it against the tree. "Cora, what are you doing here?" he asked, trying to hide that he was surprised to see her.

"I saw you leave camp, and I just thought I would come to find you," she said, her voice shaking slightly. "I'm sorry for interrupting you." She turned to leave, but he moved toward her.

"Wait," he said. "You don't have to apologize. I was just . . . trying to get some more firewood, and this tree . . . well, it was determined to stay in the ground." He chuckled as his gaze danced around then he clenched his jaw.

She wanted to look at him but couldn't. "Oh. I thought perhaps you were hitting it because you were angry at something."

"Well, I was, but it was at the tree."

"That makes sense." Cora chewed on her lip, then clasped her hands at her waist in front of her. She took a deep breath and walked towards Sam. She could feel his eyes on her, burning a hole into her skin. She tried to push away her doubts and hesitations, but they only seemed to grow stronger with each passing minute that neither of them said a word. "I suppose I should let you get back to chopping wood." She finally managed to say, her voice barely above a whisper.

Sam raised an eyebrow. "Perhaps we could stand together for the church service before we leave camp tomorrow morning."

Cora shrugged, feeling a blush creeping up her neck. She thought they could spend the afternoon together or at least share supper. But instead of suggesting it, she simply smiled and nodded. "That would be lovely." She took a step back, feeling the weight of his words. She didn't know what to say, but their awkwardness seemed to stretch forever.

Finally, Sam let out a sigh and rubbed his face with his hands. "Look, Cora. I'm sorry if I scared you. It's just that . . . I have a lot on my mind right now. And the tree was proving rather difficult." He chuckled again, and while there was a hint of authenticity to it, she also felt as though he did it more to smooth over her feelings and make light of the whole situation.

Cora nodded, still unsure of what to say. "It's all right. I understand. We are all allowed moments of anger. Even I have been known to have outbursts a time or two."

"What? You? I can't see it." He offered her a huge smile that seemed to ease her mind slightly. "You'll have to tell me what got you so mad later."

"Oh, I'm not sure I can even remember. It was probably something you'd find silly, like another girl stealing my dress or a boy pulling on one of my braids."

"All the more reasons for me to hear the story." His voice softened. "Thank you for following me. You being here . . . it eases my mind."

She felt her heart flutter at his words. It was the glint of something she had needed to help her. "I can stay and help you with the wood. If you would like."

He shook his head. "There's no need. I'm sure your headmistress could use your help in getting the wagon packed."

"Oh. All right." She didn't know whether to hide her disappointment or not, but in the end, she did, or at least she tried. The whole situation and his dismissiveness were awkward enough; she didn't want to make it any more so. "You're probably right. I know Winona could use the help."

"I'll see you in the morning," he said, a small smile tugging at his lips' corners.

∼

Cora emerged from the trees. Her mind reeled from the last few moments. She didn't know what to make of any of it—Sam and his behavior, the things he'd said. She clutched her chest, trying to slow her breathing down. The more she tried, however, the more she pictured Sam chopping at the wood with such fervor that it seemed like he was trying to kill it. Every strike of his ax against the tree trunk sent splinters flying in all directions, and the sound of his angry grunts echoed through the brush. She felt a sense of unease settle in her chest as she watched him continue his furious assault on the tree. Clearly, he was taking out his frustrations on the helpless tree, and the thought of what might be causing his anger sent a shiver down her spine.

What had caused Sam to be so angry?

No matter how much she tried, she couldn't shake the image of his angry face out of her mind. She had never seen him like that before, and the intensity of his every movement had left her unsettled.

She would have liked to have asked a little more about what was bothering him or at least let him know she was more than willing to listen if he wanted someone to talk to. But, of course, that was even if he was the type to speak to a woman about things that were bothering him. Part of her wondered if he was or not, and since he hadn't seemed too interested in doing so earlier...

Did that mean he wasn't?

Her heart sank at the thought of him telling her to return to the wagon and help pack. She had hoped to spend more time with him, to get to know him better, but it seemed like he was pushing her away. Was it something she had done? Had she made a wrong choice in going after him?

What did that mean for them? Were they not meant to be together?

No, she thought. *It couldn't be. They had to be meant for one another. I want love and marriage, and I don't want to wait any longer.*

Despite her questions and how he'd been, she knew she couldn't just give up on Sam. She cared for him too profoundly to simply walk away, and she was determined to try and figure out what was going on with him. She would stand by him, no matter what, and she would do everything she could to help him through whatever was causing his anger.

As she approached the wagon, she took a deep breath and shoved the whole afternoon from her mind. She knew that she needed to be strong for Sam, which meant putting her feelings aside for the time being. She would be there for him, no matter what, and she would do everything she could to help him through his troubles.

No matter what, I will help him.

As she approached the wagon, Winona stormed around the wagon, tossing several blankets on the ground. Dust clouded around the material, and she growled.

"Winona? What happened? Is everything all right?"

Winona let out another growl. "It's that blasted Mr. Mills."

"What about him?"

"He makes me so mad. I swear, he makes my blood boil, and that's what's wrong." The headmistress stomped one foot as she clenched her hands into fists. They shook at her side. Cora had seen the woman mad several times growing up. She was no stranger to the screams she could hear down the hallway when children wouldn't listen or do as they were told. Of course, the woman wasn't overly cruel or a bear to live with. She was a like a parent reprimanding their children—or at least Cora thought that was how parents were.

So, while it wasn't abnormal to see the woman mad, this was probably the maddest Cora had seen her.

What was with today? Why was everyone on such edge?

"I swear that man . . . he's just not a good man, and he's an even worse wagon master."

"What did he do?"

"I asked him for advice on a particular situation, and he was completely unhelpful."

"What kind of advice did you ask for?" Cora inquired cautiously.

Winona whipped her head toward Cora and opened her mouth. Before she answered, however, she stopped herself. She hesitated for a moment before answering. "It's not important," she said, dismissively waving a hand. "What's important is that he's not doing his job properly, and it's affecting all of us."

Cora nodded, not wanting to push the issue. She could tell that Winona was in a bad mood and didn't want to make things worse. She shifted her weight from one foot to the other, unsure what to say next.

Winona blew out a breath and shook her head. "I don't want to think about it anymore, nor do I want to waste my time on that man. How was your visit with Mr. Wright?"

A lump formed in Cora's throat, and although she tried to swallow it, she couldn't. She didn't want to tell Winona about what she had just witnessed in the forest. She didn't want to betray Sam's trust or make him look bad in front of their headmistress, even if she couldn't shake the image of Sam's angry face out of her head. "Fine," she muttered, half choking. "He needed to chop some firewood, so he asked if we could stand together at the church service tomorrow morning before we leave."

"That's nice."

"Yeah."

"Well, I suppose we should start packing. Harper and Grace will be back from the river soon. Or at least I hope they will. Knowing those two, who knows how long they will take to bathe and wash their hair." Winona rolled her eyes and then closed them, exhaling a breath. "I didn't mean that to sound as cruel as it did. I need to let the whole thing with Mr. Mills go."

Although Cora wanted to tell the headmistress she knew exactly how the woman felt, she didn't. Instead, she nodded and bit her tongue, hoping and praying that tomorrow she would see a different Sam Wright and that the Sam Wright she saw today would never make another appearance ever again.

SIX

JASPER

"Fear," Preacher Levinson's voice echoed above those gathered for service in the early morning hours, and the sound jolted Jasper from his thoughts. "We all have it. We all live through it, and some of us even live by it, letting it control how we act, the things we say, and the choices we make. But, should we allow it such authority over our lives?"

The preacher paused, looking at several faces as though he looked to find those willing to answer his question aloud. No one did, and while Jasper considered shouting something out for a second, he didn't. Something stopped him, and while he didn't know what it was, he figured it was because he knew that if his mama had been around, she would have smacked him on the back of the head.

It was funny how she still had that power over him.

Or maybe it wasn't a power, but it was more that he didn't want to disappoint her, even if he knew she would never know what he'd done.

"We have had our fearful times on this journey. We've dealt with loss and suffering. We've dealt with the hardships of storms, disease, and rivers that we didn't know if we would make it. But through it all, we have always had Him. He watches over us and protects us. He gives us strength. He provides."

Jasper tightened his coat around his neck, warding off the chill in the early morning air. He hadn't been particularly fond of rising early this morning after a long afternoon and evening of gold panning, and after finding nothing, he also hadn't been in the greatest of moods either.

"*Psalm 27:1–3* says, The Lord is my light and my salvation; whom shall I fear? The Lord is the stronghold of my life; of whom shall I be afraid? When evildoers assail me to eat up my flesh, my adversaries and foes, it is they who stumble and fall. Though an army encamps against me, my heart shall not fear; though war arises against me, yet I will be confident. It is with this verse that I ask you, what have you not been confident in? Can you change it? Ask yourselves what you could do to not be afraid and to live knowing that the Lord is the stronghold of your life?"

As the preacher paused to let everyone think about what he'd asked, a few people in the crowd glanced around at one another as if they were thinking about the answers to the preacher's questions. Husbands looked at their wives and then at one another, all while Jasper stood in the back, watching and thinking.

There were several things in life he'd always been sure of. Farming, certainly, was one of them. He could probably plant and take care of crops in his sleep. He knew what soil they needed, how much sunlight and water were best suited for them, and when to harvest for peak freshness. Gold panning was another. Well, not so much when he started, of course, but as he learned about how to read the river for the best spot and how to swirl the pan in the exact way he needed, he knew that when he reached California, all of his gold-finding dreams would come true. He was sure of it.

He was confident about it.

So what was it that he wasn't confident about, he thought, snorting a slight laugh at the answer. *Women.*

Women had been one thing he hadn't ever been confident in. Even as a young boy and while growing into a young man, he'd never found the courage to truly open himself up and let someone get close to him. Even when his mama tried to introduce him to a lovely lady, the feeling of love was something he had never quite understood. He couldn't comprehend how two people could care so deeply for one another that they were willing to make sacrifices for each other and lay down their own lives if need be. He almost found this concept terrifying yet beautiful at the same time, and it made him feel small in comparison.

"I ask you, what have you not been confident in? Can you change it? Ask yourselves what you could do to not be afraid and to live knowing that the Lord is the stronghold of your life?"

The preacher's words repeated in Jasper's mind, and for the first time, Jasper wondered if his lack of understanding hadn't really been about the feelings but more about the women themselves. Did he fear love and marriage? Or did he fear women?

Did that even make sense, he wondered.

"I know that the road can be difficult," the preacher continued. "I know that the devil likes to creep into your minds, telling you that whatever it is you seek is impossible and to hang onto your fear because it will keep you safe. But don't listen. For God was calling you to have faith—faith in Him and faith in His plan for your life. No matter what happens, you will find your strength in knowing that the Lord is your light and your salvation—a strong fortress you may turn to when everything else seems uncertain or overwhelming."

Jasper snorted again. Yeah. Overwhelming. That was how he felt about women.

He looked through the back of everyone's heads, trying to ignore that he was searching for the one woman in particular who had invaded his thoughts more often since yesterday than he cared to admit—Miss Cora Randall. It wasn't that he didn't want to think about her, it was just that he couldn't get her out of his mind, and while he wanted to fight them, he failed more often than not. This morning had been even worse as they gathered for the service, and he caught himself searching for her a few times.

"If we go on to read *Psalm 27:4-6*, it says, one thing have asked of the Lord," the preacher continued, "that will I seek after that I may dwell in the house of the Lord all the days of my life, to gaze upon the beauty of the Lord and to inquire in his temple. For he will hide me in his shelter in the day of trouble; he will conceal me under the cover of his tent; he will lift me high upon a rock. And now my head shall be lifted up above my enemies all around me, and I will offer in his tent sacrifices with shouts of joy; I will sing and make melody to the Lord. Let us pray..."

As Preacher Levinson lifted the Bible in his hand, everyone in the wagon train bowed their heads.

"Father in Heaven, we have humbly gathered together this morning to ask for Your continued blessings. We all know that life is not without strife and hardship, but we ask that You keep Your watchful eye upon us, helping us through the trials we will encounter on this trail. We also ask that You watch over our wagon master, giving him the wisdom to get us through all we might face. We pray this in Jesus' name. Amen."

"Amen," the crowd said after him.

The sun had just begun to rise over the mountains in the distance, painting the sky in brilliant hues of red and orange. It was as though God wanted to give them hope—or at least give him hope—and as the people dispersed and headed back to their wagons as Mr. Mills had ordered, Jasper noticed Miss Randall standing near a wagon. Her silhouette captivated him in the rising sunlight, and as he looked upon her, he thought of their conversation by the river and the sermon at this morning's service. He wished he had been more confident the other morning instead of allowing the unmistakable anxiety to linger just enough to make him wonder if he'd been a fool.

Had he said anything wrong?

Was that why she didn't want to go with him downriver?

His brow furrowed, and before he could turn away, Cora caught his eye. She smiled and waved, sending warmth to spread through his body. For a moment, he forgot all of his worries, and he wanted nothing more than to talk to her again. The only problem was mustering up the courage to approach her.

He had to do it.

Just walk toward her, he thought. *And don't stop.*

His heart thumped. He was going to do it. He was going to walk over to her and talk to her. He hadn't stopped thinking about her, and even though love and marriage weren't in his plans, he just had to know her, had to spend time with her. He didn't know why.

He only knew he had to.

Call it gut intuition—as Mama called it. Like when you know something was put on this earth just for you. That's how he felt. She was put on this earth for him.

Just like gold.

He began walking toward her, but before he could take more than just a few steps, however, another man stepped up beside her and laid his hand on her shoulder. He leaned into her, whispering something in her ear, and as Cora looked over at him, Jasper finally took notice of the other man too. Recognition instantly flashed through his mind—it was the same man who had been bothering the Doctor's wife yesterday morning.

Jasper sucked in a breath as the man, and Cora exchanged glances that seemed far more intimate than what Jasper was comfortable with. He stopped walking and watched them.

Confusion, anger, jealousy, and fear all swirled within him at once.

What was Miss Randall doing with him, Jasper wondered. *Does she not know the type of man he is?*

A burn of frustration warmed through him, and his insides twisted as he imagined her with that man. He didn't like the idea of her picking someone like that, but at the same time, he knew it was not his place to butt in, even if the thought of staying quiet and watching her make a terrible mistake made him feel sick to his stomach.

Why did she have to be with him?

Mr. Wright leaned in, whispering in Cora's ear again.

Jasper sucked in another breath and moved toward them.

He wasn't about to stand by any longer.

~

CORA

Cora watched as Jasper made his way through the crowd in her direction. She had seen him before, of course, but this time he was different—more confident, more sure of himself. It was like he felt the purpose of the sermon that Preacher Levinson just gave, and his strides were as steady and as sure as a locomotive on its tracks. Her heart thumped. She wanted to tell him to stop, yet at the same time, she didn't. Paralyzed, she hesitated between her desire to talk to him and the fear of how she would feel if she did.

"It was a nice service, wasn't it?" Sam's voice echoed in Cora's ear and jerked her attention.

"Huh?" She looked at him, cocking one eyebrow.

"I asked you if you thought it was a nice service."

"Oh. Yes. It was. Although, I think all of Preacher Levinson's sermons are lovely." She looked back toward Jasper, who was still approaching her. A slight chuckled breath left her lips. He really did have a cute way about him, even if he looked slightly angry.

"Good morning, Miss Randall," Jasper said.

"Good morning, Mr. Scott."

As she nodded toward him, he looked at Sam and stuck his hand out. "Good morning. I don't believe we had the pleasure of meeting the other day. I'm Mr. Jasper Scott."

The other day? Cora's head jerked slightly. *What did that mean?*

"Mr. Sam Wright." Sam blew out a breath as he shook Jasper's hand. Their fists clenched together so tight Cora could see their arms tremble as though they were straining. Although Sam looked in Jasper's direction, he didn't make eye contact.

"It's nice to meet you, Mr. Wright. Since we weren't able to make each other's acquaintance the other day." Jasper gave Sam's hand another hard jerk, then released it, turning his attention toward Cora, clasping his hands behind his back. "It was a lovely sermon this morning, wasn't it?"

Before Cora could even open her mouth to answer, Sam spoke instead. "We were just talking about how nice we thought it was." His voice carried a hint of growl to it, and Cora blinked at him.

Just what was going on between these two?

"Oh, ya were, were ya? Well, it's nice to hear that you two talk about things. Hopefully, you talk about many, many things —especially matters that happen around the camp." Jasper smiled for a moment, then his eyes narrowed, and he glared at Sam.

Cora looked at Winona, Harper, and Grace, who watched the whole scene looking as perplexed about Jasper's choice of words as she was.

Why would he say something like that?

"We talk about enough," Sam said. He squared his chest and

cleared his throat, staring at Jasper until Winona jumped between the two men, distracting them both.

"We should probably get to our wagons. I'm sure Mr. Mills will want to leave now that the service is over." She looked at both men several times as though she waited for them to take her hint and leave.

Jasper glanced down at the ground and then at her, nodding. "You're right, Ma'am. We should." He tipped his hat to the four women and then looked at Sam, a sly smirk spread across his face as if he was pleased to have gotten under Sam's skin. Sam, for his part, seemed only to get madder, and Cora brushed her fingers across her collarbone as she prayed he would not explode into the fits of anger she knew he was capable of.

Before Sam could do anything, though, Winona grabbed Cora's arm and tugged her away from the two men. Although she wanted to look over her shoulder at them, she didn't.

She didn't have the courage to.

"What was that all about?" Harper asked, trotting after Cora and Winona.

"I don't know." Winona shook her head. Her jaw clenched for a second. "But it seems to me that Cora doesn't just have one suitor vying for her attention. It seems as though she has two."

"Two?" Cora blinked at the headmistress. "But Jasper isn't ... he's headed to California and has plans to leave the wagon train after Fort Hall. He's not looking to get married."

"A man's plans can change," Winona said. "Especially when the likes of a woman catches his eye. He wouldn't have acted that way if he didn't have any interest in getting to know you."

The four women reached their wagon, and the headmistress motioned for Cora, Harper, and Grace to climb inside, and while Grace and Harper made their way to the back, Cora and Winona scrambled up onto the buckboard.

"Who do you think you like the most, Cora?" Grace asked,

raising one eyebrow as she settled in the back of the wagon and tucked her skirt under her legs.

"Yeah. I'm curious to know too." Harper nestled next to Grace and leaned against the trunk, lifting her arm and resting her elbow on a trunk.

"I don't know." She looked over her shoulder and around the side of the wagon, watching as the two men finally walked away from one another, returning to their wagons so they were ready to leave. She didn't know if anything was said between them after she left, but part of her didn't want to know if there was. Surely, it wasn't anything a proper woman should hear. "I just don't know."

"Well, if I were you, I would try to make a decision." Winona grabbed the reins and slapped them on the horses' backs. "And I wouldn't wait too long."

"Why?"

Winona laughed. "Because those two are fit to come to blows if you do."

SEVEN

CORA

Throughout the rest of the day and the next, Cora's body swayed as the wagon rolled down the trail. Mile after mile, they crossed the Nebraska countryside, and while she looked out across the horizon, watching the tall grass flutter in the breeze, nothing seemed to resonate in her mind.

As a young girl, she dreamed of having more than one man vying for her attention and affection. She would dance around her room at the orphanage, pretending to attend a dance with a full dance card and men waiting in line. She thought it would be wonderful to have options and be able to choose from a pool of suitors, and she imagined herself being pursued relentlessly, with her heart fluttering at the thought of their affections.

Of course, each one had been a mystery man. Just pictured images in her head of men she'd see on the street or versions of them. Some were tall. Some were short. Some were built with a thinner frame like Sam, while others, like Jasper, had a stoutness that seemed to engulf her petite size. It was always the one thing she loved about being short—having men towering over her. She felt protected, and the thought filled her with the sense of security she never had as a child. It was comforting, and she allowed herself to forget about the pain and heartbreak she had known before leaving Missouri in search of love and adventure.

But now, as she traveled alone in the wagon, her thoughts turned to the men she had known in real life, and as she found herself amid the very situation she thought she dreamed about, she realized that it was not as great as she once thought. It was emotionally draining, confusing, and downright overwhelming. She had two men, Jasper and Sam, who were equally interested in her—or at least such was what Winona thought; Cora still was unsure of Jasper's intentions. But still, even if the headmistress was right . . .

Cora didn't know who to choose.

"At least it's a lovely day to travel." Winona sighed a deep breath, glancing at Cora as the wagon continued down the trail.

"I suppose. The sun is bright, though." Cora squinted as she looked at the blue sky. There wasn't a cloud in sight. "And without any clouds, it will get hot."

"You're more than welcome to move to the back."

"I'd rather be here. It's too bouncy back there. It makes me sick to my stomach." A slight growl hinted through Cora's words.

"Suit yourself." Winona tapped the reins on the horses' backs, not that it mattered much. They weren't going to go any faster than the wagon before them. "So . . ." The woman hesitated. "Have you thought about what you will do?"

"About?"

"Mr. Scott and Mr. Wright?"

"No."

"I suppose I shouldn't be surprised by the turn of events." Winona chuckled. "Out of all of you, I knew that you would be the one to have more than one man wanting your attention."

"To be honest, it was something I had hoped for."

"Oh, I don't doubt that."

"Neither do we," Harper said from the back. She poked her

head through the bonnet and laughed as she shielded her eyes from the sun's bright rays.

Cora whipped her head toward the woman. "And just what is that supposed to mean?"

"Oh, come on, Cora. You've always been the one who has wanted the most attention, and you know it. In fact, you have often boasted about it."

Cora opened her mouth to argue but said nothing as she couldn't find anything to say. She knew she'd always talked about wanting more than one man's attention, and while she wished she could take back all those times, she knew she couldn't.

"All right. Fine. I admit it. I've always wanted all the attention. So there. Are you happy?" she asked Harper.

"A little."

"What else do you wish for me to say? That it was foolish of me, and I know this now? Because it was. Having more than one man . . . it's not fun, and I can't believe that I thought it would be."

"You better not let Lark ever hear you say such things. She won't ever let you live it down." Harper winked, then vanished behind the bonnet. Cora could hear her and Grace giggle, and she rolled her eyes.

"Aside from all that," Winona said, shaking her head, "which I will not comment on. How do you feel about the two men?"

"I don't know." Cora looked out of the horizon, picturing them both in her mind.

On the one hand, there's Jasper. He was kind and gentle, and in the short time they'd spent together, he'd made her laugh and feel as though he'd fight the world if she asked. She felt safe and comfortable around him, like she could tell him anything, and he wouldn't bat an eye. But on the other hand, there was Sam. He was charming, spontaneous, and had an air of mystery about him that she found alluring—or at least a little. At times he confused her more than anything.

"I find myself torn between the two, and my mind is in a constant battle of tug-of-war. Whenever I think I could choose one, doubt creeps in, and I second-guess myself."

"They both seem like nice men, even if they also don't seem to like one another."

"They are. But they are different. And I don't even know how Jasper feels. The way that he spoke of his future and California. I don't think he wants to get married."

"Then it sounds like Sam will give you what you want."

"Yes, it does."

"But?"

"But what if I make the wrong choice? What if I hurt one of them? What if I end up alone?"

"I highly doubt that would happen."

Although Cora wanted to believe her headmistress, there was still a weight on her shoulders dragging her down enough to make her feel like she was drowning. She knew she needed to decide soon, but she couldn't shake off the uncertainty. She never thought having two men vying for her attention would feel like a burden instead of a blessing.

Maybe it wasn't the men themselves that were the problem, but the pressure that came with making a choice. She didn't want to hurt anyone's feelings or make the wrong decision.

"I just wish there was a way to know for sure which one is right for me," she said.

Winona laid her hand on Cora's shoulder. "When the time comes, you will."

"Are you certain of that?"

"I am."

The wagon in front of theirs stopped, and Winona jerked the horses to a halt. Dust clouded around them, and although it did little to help, Cora waved her hand in front of her face. She coughed a few times, then covered her nose and mouth with her hand.

"Why did we stop?" she asked.

"I don't know." Winona hooked the reins around the buckboard and climbed down. She brushed at her skirt, then looked up at the girls as Harper and Grace peeked out from under the bonnet. "Stay here while I see why we stopped."

"We should come with you," Harper said.

Winona lifted her finger, wiggling it toward the young woman. "Just stay here." Her voice had that parent bite to it as though to warn Harper that they would find themselves in trouble if they didn't listen to her. Cora glanced at Harper, who looked as though she wanted to argue again but didn't, and the three women watched the headmistress vanish in the dust.

The heat pounded down on the back of Cora's neck, and the more she watched people pass the wagon on foot, the more she felt an anxious itch crawl up her skin. She didn't like sitting around, waiting. She wanted to know what had happened.

"Where are you going?" Harper asked as Cora climbed down from the wagon.

The dust had cleared slightly, but the women still waved their hands in front of their faces as though it helped. Cora shrugged, and a thin line appeared between her eyes as she glanced around them at the hustle and bustle. "To find out what happened," she said.

"But Winona said for us to stay here."

"I don't care. I'm not waiting any longer." Cora trudged off, not waiting to see if the other two women would follow her or not. It didn't matter if they did. She didn't need them to go with her.

Cora found Winona on the outskirts of the crowd that had formed alongside one of the wagons, and the headmistress shook her head as Cora approached.

"I knew of all of three that it would be you who wouldn't listen."

"Sorry. I couldn't take it any longer."

Winona waved her hand. "It's fine. There is nothing to be concerned with."

"So, what is going on?"

"Mr. and Mrs. Fairchild's wagon has a broken wheel, and the men are all trying to repair it." She pointed toward the wagon, and Cora adjusted her stance, peeking around Mr. and Mrs. Stonemill until she could see the Fairchild's wagon and most of the men in the wagon train huddled around the wheel.

Cora looked around for Sam but couldn't find him. She continued moving through the crowd, looking for the tall man, but seeing him nowhere, she moved back to Winona, shrugging when Winona asked her if she wanted to return to their wagon.

"I'll stay," she said.

"All right."

Winona nodded and left, and as she watched the headmistress leave, she caught sight of Jasper making his way toward the Fairchild's wagon. He held several tools in his hands, and his silhouette darkened against the sun setting behind him. With his cowboy hat pulled low over his eyes, his broad shoulders moved with a ruggedness that made her heart skip a beat, and for a moment, she thought he was nothing more than another mirage, like those she had read about in books that people see in the desert. She sucked in a breath, and as he grew closer, she could see the determination etched into his face. He nodded as he passed her, and as he approached the crowd, several wagon train members moved aside, letting him through.

Cora fought the urge to follow behind him, and she remained on the outskirts with the other women and children, who seemed more interested in running around playing than watching what their fathers were doing. A few of the wives tried to squash the children's fun by telling them to hush or go back to their wagons, and while a few of the young boys listened, others didn't, forcing their mothers to leave their perched spots in front of the crowd.

As more and more women and children left, soon there were only a handful of people watching as the men got to work unloading the wagon. Sam arrived not long after Jasper, and he nodded toward Cora before helping everyone set the Fairchild's belongings aside in the dirt and brush, not caring too much about Mrs. Fairchild standing near her precious items with tears in her eyes.

"I just don't want anything to break," she told the other women who tried to comfort her.

"Honey, if it hasn't broken riding around in the bouncy wagon, then it's not going to break just being set on the ground," Mrs. Stonemill said to her while Mrs. Reed and Mrs. Collins nodded in agreement.

Cora joined the remaining wives, watching the men work together to lift the heavy wagon, loosen the bolts, and carefully remove the broken wheel from the axle. Sweat dripped from their faces and moistened their shirts as the hot sun beat down upon them with a relentless heat that seemed to sizzle the ground around them.

With the old wheel removed, the men inspected the axle for any damage or wear, and after they seemed to deem it fine, they went to work fitting the new wheel onto the axle and tightening the bolts that held it in place.

Cora watched as Jasper rushed around, helping every chance he could and even helping Mr. Mills supervise the steps the men needed to take. He'd obviously changed a wagon wheel a time or two in his life before and was taking charge almost as if he were helping his own family, working harder than all of the other men—Sam included. A slight part of Cora wanted to take a mental note of it, but the other part of her told her not to judge. Surely, there was a reason. Perhaps Sam had never changed a wagon wheel before. There were things she hadn't done, and she would hate for someone to judge her based on her knowledge or lack thereof.

"I wonder if we will continue on or set up camp?" Mrs. Reed asked, glancing around at the other wives.

"It's hard to say. Although, with the sun starting to set, it would seem foolish to continue. We wouldn't make it far before dark anyway." Mrs. Stonemill folded her arms across her chest. " Perhaps we should tell Mr. Mills that—"

A sound rattled, and the women froze.

"What was that?" Mrs. Fairchild asked.

"I don't know." Mrs. Stonemill looked at all the women. "It sounds like a baby rattle."

The sound echoed again, and Cora looked down to the right, searching through the tall grass. A snake slithered closer to them.

"It's a snake!" she shouted.

The women screamed and scattered. Each one darted in a different direction, and in mass confusion, Mrs. Fairchild collided with Cora, knocking her to the ground. She landed with a thud, and pain shot up her back and down her legs. She heard the rattle again, and she froze as she glanced over. She'd landed mere inches from the snake, which had coiled up, tucking its rattling tail behind it. Her heart pounded, and sweat beaded the back of her neck. The snake's beady eyes were fixed on her, and it licked the air. It looked as though it could strike at any second. She knew one strike could be fatal and screamed again, looking all around for Sam. She saw him in the distance, frozen with his mouth gaped open. Although she shouted for him, he didn't move.

As the snake reared back to strike, Cora closed her eyes, waiting for the inevitable. She heard a loud grunt, the slice of what sounded like a shovel hitting the ground, and a few women screamed, and she opened her eyes as Jasper drove the tip of a shovel through the snake's body, severing its head. He twisted the tool, digging the blade further into the ground. The snake's head lay in the sand with its mouth open while the body twisted upon itself. He kicked it away, then kicked the head in a different direction. His lungs heaved, and he wiped his brow with his shirt sleeve.

She looked up at him, her heart was racing, and tears misted her eyes. She blinked them away before they could stream down her cheeks. He smiled as he offered her a hand, helping her to her feet, and she felt a rush of warmth as their hands touched. For a moment, they stood there, staring at each other, their eyes locked.

"Are you okay?" he asked, breaking the silence with his low and husky voice.

Cora nodded; her throat was tight. "I think so," she whispered. "Thank you."

Jasper smiled, and his eyes crinkled at the corners. "You're welcome."

Out of the corner of her eyes, Cora saw Winona running toward her.

"What happened?" the headmistress shouted. Before Cora could answer, the woman wrapped her arms around Cora, squeezing her in a tight hug.

"There was a snake."

"A snake? Where?" Winona glanced around.

"Jasper killed it, and he kicked it away."

Winona continued to look around the ground for a moment before she glanced up at Jasper and moved toward him, hugging him. "Thank you," she said.

"You're welcome, ma'am."

"I don't believe we've had the pleasure of meeting. I'm Winona Callahan, Cora's headmistress."

"I figured, ma'am. Mr. Jasper Scott." He ducked his chin and removed his hat from his head. "You can call me Jasper."

"Well, Jasper, it's a good thing you were around. How did you know what to do with the snake?"

"We always had snakes on the farm, ma'am."

"Well, Cora was lucky you were around then. Thank you for saving her."

"You're welcome, ma'am."

She blew out a breath, wrapping her arm around Cora's waist before she led her off to the wagon. Cora glanced over her shoulder, looking at Jasper for a moment before Sam moved to Jasper's side. She caught Sam's glare, and her stomach twisted.

∼

JASPER

Jasper watched the two women leave, feeling a knot form in his chest. Everything had happened so fast that he hadn't had a chance to even think about the snake or saving Cora. While the rest of the men returned to work repacking the Fairchild's wagon, Jasper made his way over to the snake's body, watching it still writhe as though it was alive. He thought about keeping it and skinning it as a souvenir.

"You used to have them on the farm, huh?" Sam slid up behind him with a hint of distaste in his voice.

"Yeah. They were always out in the fields."

"Well, how convenient for you, then."

"Convenient?" Jasper cocked his head to the side and furrowed his brow. He turned to face Sam, only to be met with a scowl. "And just what is that supposed to mean?" Jasper asked, trying to keep his voice even. He knew Sam had eyes for Cora, but he didn't expect Sam to approach him in the manner which he now did.

Sam crossed his arms over his chest and shot him a glare. "You know what it means. I saw how you were looking at her after the service. It was like you were biding your time until something happened, and she needed you."

Jasper's jaw clenched. "Are you implying I wanted something bad to happen to her?"

"Well, it didn't take you long to jump in and save her."

"You're right. It didn't. But it took you a long time to react. In fact, you didn't react at all."

Sam's jaw clenched, and his eyes narrowed. He stepped toward Jasper, and although Jasper got the impression he did so, thinking Jasper would retreat, Jasper didn't move. Even if Sam was a foot taller than Jasper, he was about fifty pounds less, and Jasper knew he could drop the man to the ground with just one punch.

"Don't play stupid with me," Sam said. A slight growl hissed through his voice. "I know what you're trying to do, and you need to stop. She's not meant for you. She's mine. I'm courting her, and I intend to marry her."

Jasper raised an eyebrow. "Is that so, huh? And how does she feel about that?"

"She's happy with it, so you just need to stay away from her."

"I was just doing my job."

"Your job? Is that what you call it?" Sam stepped closer, his eyes blazing. "You have no business getting involved with her."

Jasper bristled at Sam's words. "I didn't get involved with her. I was there to help."

"Help? You mean you were there to save the damsel in distress?"

Jasper took a deep breath, trying to keep his temper in check. His hands flexed into fists at his sides. He didn't appreciate Sam's tone, nor did he appreciate his insinuations. "I didn't see her as a damsel in distress. I saw her as a person who needed help."

Sam's eyes narrowed. "Just trying to play hero, then, huh? Did you happen to have Mrs. Fairchild run into Cora on purpose to knock her down, too? Well, you can't save everyone."

Jasper jerked his head, shaking it. "What are you talking about? I'm not trying to save everyone. I'm just doing what I can to help where I can."

Sam crossed his arms over his chest. "Well, I don't need your help. And neither does Cora."

Jasper shook his head. "It didn't look that way to me today, and I don't care what you think. I'll help anyone who needs it. So don't think I will stand back and let you get in the way of me doing my job."

Sam snorted, taking another step closer toward Jasper. "Your job? That's a laugh. What, do you think you are the wagon master now?"

Jasper didn't back down, and he met Sam's gaze head-on, his own eyes blazing with intensity. "That's not what I mean. I meant that Cora needed help, and I was there to provide it. End of story."

Sam's nostrils flared. "You're lying. You want her for yourself."

Jasper shook his head, his patience wearing thin. "I don't want her for myself."

"Then why were you looking at her like that?" Sam demanded.

"I wasn't looking at her in any particular way," Jasper retorted. "And even if I was, it's none of your business."

Sam's eyes narrowed, and he took another step forward until the two men were only inches apart. "Everything that concerns Cora is my business."

"Mr. Scott! Mr. Wright!" Mr. Mills shouted. "We could use the help."

While Sam locked his eyes on Jasper, Jasper turned toward the wagon master. "Be right there." He turned back to Sam. "I don't know who ya think ya are, but if you think I'm going to listen to a word of what ya have to say, you are in for a serious disappointment."

Before Sam could utter a response, Jasper trotted back to the wagon. A slight chuckle warmed through his breath. While Sam's audacity didn't shock him, he also hadn't expected it either, and now, even more than ever, he wanted to keep Cora away from such a man.

EIGHT

CORA

Cora sat by the campfire, watching the flames lick at the charred chunk of wood in the middle. Every time she closed her eyes, she saw the snake, and at times when the wood would pop and spark, the sound made her flinch. She knew she should be grateful to be alive, but all she could think of was the snake that had lunged at her just a few hours ago. She had never been so close to death, and the experience had left her feeling raw and exposed. She hardly thought about any of the women around her making supper nor about Lark and Carter, who had joined them this evening at Winona's request.

Although the woman never said why, Cora believed she wanted all the girls close after what happened this afternoon. Part of Cora thought the woman was crazy to even feel as though she did. What did it matter if they were all together or not? It didn't make anything go away.

In fact, it only made the memories worse, and each time they flashed through Cora's mind, her heart would race, and her stomach would churn. She tried to calm herself by focusing on the fire. Its warmth was welcome in the cool evening air, and its soft light was like a balm to her rattled nerves.

When she was ten years old, she'd been stung by a bee, and although she didn't know how a snake bite would feel, she imagined it would be worse than the bee sting. Not to mention a lot more deadly.

"Do people die from snake bites?" Lark asked Carter as she sat next to him across the campfire from Cora. She had a bowl of stew in her hands, and she tucked it into her lap, dipping her spoon inside and scooping up a bite. She blew on the hot supper before shoving it in her mouth.

Cora shot her a glare, hissing a slight breath.

"What?" Lark looked at her, blinking. "It's an honest question."

"And one I would think you would already know the answer to, Mrs. Doctor Evans." Cora's words bit through the air, and although she should have felt awful for her tone, she didn't. It was a foolish question, and she knew Lark asked it on purpose.

"What is wrong with you? Just because I'm married to a doctor doesn't mean I know everything about the practice of medicine." Lark furrowed her brow and cocked her head to the side.

Carter glanced between the two women and cleared his throat. "Did you still want the answer?" he asked his wife.

"Of course I do." She scowled at Cora.

"Well, the answer is yes, it can. Although, I have to say there have been cases—and lots of them—where the victim survives."

"And how do you know if the person will live?"

"It depends on the bite location. Say, someone gets a bite on their leg or arm. Well, it might not be as bad if one can get the poison out and remove the limb in time with an amputation before it spreads through the bloodstream."

Harper and Grace sat on the other side of him, and a shudder ran down Harper's back. She shivered, nearly dropping her bowl of stew. "Please don't mention blood," she whispered.

"What's the matter?" Carter chuckled. "Don't like the word?"

"The word. The sight of it. Even the thought of it." She shivered again. "I just can't."

He chuckled again. "Forgive me, then. I won't mention it again."

Winona was the last to sit down and she tucked the bowl tight in her hand, stirring the hot meal with her spoon for a moment before taking a bite.

"Well, I'm just glad nothing happened. But if it had, I'm happy you would have known what to do, Carter."

Cora rolled her eyes. She didn't know how much more of the conversation she could take. Did none of them care that she'd been through something this afternoon? She could have been bitten, for Pete's sake. She glanced around the fire. Part of her felt bad for even feeling annoyed; surely, they didn't mean any harm. But whether they did or didn't, it didn't matter. She couldn't take it anymore.

She had to leave.

She shot to her feet, brushing the dirt, grass, and rocks from her skirt. "Excuse me," she said, not bothering to look at anyone nor stop when Winona asked where she was going.

"Just let her go," she heard Lark say to the headmistress. "She probably just needs some time to herself."

Shockingly enough, for once, she could agree with Lark.

Although Cora didn't want to meander too far from the wagons, nor did she like the thought of walking through the tall grass down to the river, she also knew the farther she could get away from the wagon, the better, so she headed down toward the river, watching every step she took and searching the grass for any other snakes that could be lurking in the shadows.

Her steps were light through the grass, and she held her breath until she reached the sandy riverbank along the water's edge. A hint of relief washed through her, and she wrapped her arms around her waist.

All she wanted to do was forget about the day and yet the

day was all she could think about. It wasn't just the snake, either. But it was Jasper and Sam and their actions when she faced trouble. While Jasper had reacted swiftly, jumping to her aid and protecting her without hesitation, Sam had frozen as though he was far too consumed by fear to do anything. She didn't want to believe that he was that type of man—unable to protect his own, yet she couldn't deny the doubt she felt about him. Did he often find himself too scared to jump in the face of danger?

A twig snapped behind her, and she spun, her heel dug into the sand, making a crescent-shaped print.

Jasper held up his hands. "I'm sorry. I didn't mean to frighten you," he said.

"It's all right. I must admit that even if I knew you were coming, I'm so jumpy that I probably would have flinched anyway."

"I just wanted to see how you were doing." He offered a slight smile as though he meant to provide comfort.

"I'm all right."

"I'm sorry about what happened."

"It's not your fault."

"I know. But I'm still sorry. I know the feeling of hearing that rattle and not knowing what will happen."

"Have you ever been bitten?" Having heard what Carter said, she knew it was a stupid question. Yet, she asked it anyway.

Jasper shook his head. "Nah. But I've had several close calls. One bit a fence post, thinking it was my boot. That was probably the closest I've had."

"It sounds like it. I can't imagine."

He shrugged. "Well, I'm glad to hear you are all right."

"Yeah. I am." She crossed her arms, hugging herself. "Thanks to you."

"It was nothing."

"It wasn't nothing, Jasper. You didn't hesitate. You saved me from an unknown fate. If the snake would have bitten me . . . I don't know what would have happened."

"Anyone would have jumped in."

"But not anyone did. You did. All the other men . . . you jumped to action, and I thank you."

He ducked his chin toward his chest, nodding, and although he tried to hide it, Cora could swear that his face flushed with a light shade of pink. Although it warmed her heart to see him slightly embarrassed, she didn't want to make him uncomfortable, so she pretended not to notice.

"Cora?" a voice shouted in the distance. "Cora!"

Before she could answer, Sam trotted through the grass toward them, and as he approached them and noticed Jasper, his face twisted with a fiery annoyance that only seemed to bubble the closer he got to them. He looked between the two, and he clenched his hands into fists.

"What are you doing here?" he asked Jasper.

"I just came to see how she was."

"But I told you to stay away from her."

Cora's face scrunched. What on earth was going on between them? And what did Sam say? "You told him what?" she asked Sam. Her brow furrowed.

"I told him to stay away from you."

"Why?"

"Because we're together, and there is no reason for him to be around you."

Cora shook her head. Of course, she understood what Sam was saying; however, she wasn't about to tell Jasper to leave her alone, not after what he'd done this afternoon. He'd saved her life. Surely, that allowed him to talk to her and ask her how she was doing. "I'm sorry. I suppose I'm a little confused. Mr. Scott was only checking to see how I was feeling. That's all."

"I don't care."

Cora stared at Sam. She didn't know what else to say. The

whole situation utterly confused her, and she also felt as though he was somewhat accusing her of improper behavior.

Was she, though, she wondered.

She backed away from both of the men. "I think I should return to my wagon."

"I'll walk you back," Sam said.

She looked at him, wanting to say no, but something stopped her.

"Cora?" Jasper looked at her, shaking his head as he rested his hands on his hips and cocked one leg out. A light growl vibrated through his breath. "You don't have to go. Not if you don't want to."

"And you need to stop talking to her." Sam moved toward Jasper, but Cora darted between them, laying her hands on Sam's chest. She didn't know what to make of the situation, but she was determined not to let it escalate like Winona had warned her it would if she took too long to decide between the two men.

"Can you take me back to my wagon," she asked him.

Sam shot another glare at Jasper before looking down at her. His hard stare softened slightly, and he nodded, backing away a few steps before turning to leave. Although she wanted to look back at Jasper, she didn't, and she followed Sam away from the river, listening to the sound of the water vanishing the farther she walked away.

As they walked, Sam kept a hand on the small of her back, guiding her through the grass. She could feel the heat emanating from his body, and it made her feel a little bit safe, despite the tension that still lingered between the two of them. She walked beside him in silence, and her mind raced with thoughts about what had just happened.

"How are you feeling after this afternoon," Sam finally asked. His voice had changed, and any annoyance he'd once felt had disappeared.

"I'm all right." She turned her face slightly in his direction but didn't look at him fully.

"Mr. Scott sure thinks highly of himself for what he did. Although, I don't think it was anything that any man wouldn't have done. Including me."

"And yet he was the one who did it."

As soon as the words slipped from Cora's lips, she regretted them, and she closed her eyes, bracing against a wrath she believed was coming.

Sam grabbed her wrist, yanking her around to face him. "Is that what he has led you to believe? That no other man on this wagon train would have protected you?"

"You're hurting me," she whispered.

He released her wrist and held his hands up. "I didn't mean to hurt you. It's just that . . . you can't trust Mr. Scott. And it would be best if you didn't believe a word he says."

"Why?"

"Because I don't want him to take you from me. That night we first talked, I knew we were meant for a great life together, and I want to live it. I don't want to lose it, and when I see him threatening that . . . I don't want anything to happen to you, especially another man trying to take you."

"He's not trying to take me from you."

"I don't believe that, and I still don't trust him. I don't think you should either." Sam lifted his hand to his face, rubbing the side. He pressed his fingers into his skin so much that his fingertips turned white. "This is all Mrs. Fairchild's fault."

"Mrs. Fairchild? What did she do?"

"She ran into you and knocked you down. If she hadn't done that, you could have gotten away." A crease formed on his forehead, and his jaw clenched as the annoyance he had when he was around Jasper returned.

Cora's heart thumped. "I don't think it was her fault. She

panicked, just as everyone did. I could have just as easily tripped and fell."

"Still. She should have been paying attention."

Cora shrugged. "We all should have."

Sam said nothing in return but looked off into the distance as though he was lost in thought. While part of her expected him to soften again, she couldn't deny that she wasn't surprised when he didn't. He was on edge, and it probably would take a night of sleep to ease the tension that obviously burdened him.

"I should get some rest. It's getting late, and we leave early in the morning."

"All right."

"Thank you for checking on me."

"Of course."

She smiled, then left him standing near the camp, heading back to her wagon with a weight on her shoulders. She knew she needed to decide which man she would choose, but the pressure and ongoing war between Jasper and Sam was becoming too much for her to handle. She didn't want to hurt either of them, but she knew she would, and she didn't want to admit that she felt drawn to both. Even if Sam had a few qualities that set her on edge, she had seen the sweet side of the tall man she'd just left, and she knew that he was only trying to help her.

"In a perfect world, I would know which one I wanted more," she said to herself. "Yet this isn't the perfect world I wish it were."

NINE

WINONA

*E*arly morning mist hovered above the river, casting a mystical calm that caused Winona to inhale a deep breath. The water was still, reflecting the soft pink and orange hues starting to glint in the dull grayness of the dawn. The sunrise was set to paint the sky above in a radiance of color, and there was a part of Winona that couldn't wait to see it. A gentle breeze rustled the leaves of the trees that lined the riverbank, creating a soothing rustling sound that blended harmoniously with the distant chirping of birds. The air was cool and crisp, carrying the sweet scent of blooming flowers, and the tall grass by the water's edge danced and swayed.

"It's a lovely morning," Winona said, dunking the bucket into the crystal-clear water. The movement blurred the colorful mosaic rocks and pebbles littering the bottom. Even if she was tired—having not slept well after yesterday—she could still find some enjoyment in her favorite time of the day.

"I suppose." Cora shrugged and then hunched her shoulders. A pout inched across her lips, and she tightened the wrap around her shoulders.

Winona watched the young woman, knowing she hadn't had

the best night's sleep either. For each time Winona tossed and turned, she could hear Cora's restlessness throughout the night too. Winona couldn't even pretend she didn't know what was on the young woman's mind. Only a fool wouldn't know.

The two women continued washing off the pans, plates, and utensils, rinsing the remnants of breakfast and letting the crumbs float down the river. Occasionally a fish would pop out from the rocks, grabbing bits of biscuits that floated nearby and caused ripples that spread outward in concentric circles.

"Thank you for your help with the dishes this morning. I just knew it would take too long if I did it myself. I always fear Mr. Mills' wrath if we aren't ready when he wants to leave." A slight chuckle hinted through her words. She mostly talked to get a reaction out of Cora than to have a conversation.

"You're welcome."

Winona watched the young woman for a moment, inhaling another deep breath. She knew she would have to rip the bandage off the wound and ask what was bothering Cora. But knowing she had to didn't mean she wanted to.

I'll give it another few minutes, she thought.

As the sun rose higher in the sky, its golden rays pierced through the mist, gradually lifting the veil of fog that had shrouded the river. The sunlight illuminated the vibrant greenery, infusing it with a warm glow that contrasted beautifully with the cool tones of the water. A lone heron landed on the other side of the river and waded down into the water, its long neck extended as it patiently waited for its prey to appear.

"I don't think you would see that in Independence," Winona said, chuckling as she pointed toward the bird. As Cora looked up, a lock of hair fell in her face, and she blew it a few times before moving it out of her face with her hand. Her breaths proved useless against the hair but had managed to scare the bird, and the two women watched it fly away.

Winona waited for Cora to say something, but she didn't.

Instead, she returned to work, scrubbing the bacon grease from a pan.

I suppose it is now or never, Winona thought.

She inhaled another deep breath. "I haven't thought much about home lately. I mean, I did in the first few weeks and a lot after Lark got sick with the measles, but I haven't thought about it much—especially since the wedding." She paused, glancing at Cora, who still hadn't looked up from the pan. "I did think about it last night, though, and I thought about how our lives would be different if we'd stayed." She paused again. "Have you thought of home?"

Cora shrugged. "I suppose I have."

"Do you miss it?"

"Sometimes. But I know that home wouldn't have been home."

"What do you mean?"

"Well, we wouldn't have been able to stay at the orphanage, so while it was my home, it wouldn't have been for long."

"Good point." Winona bit her lip and then continued. "Still, though, home or not, it probably would be a lot safer." She snorted a laugh. "Actually, I know it would be a lot safer. I guess that's why I thought of it. I worry about what I've brought upon you, Harper, Grace, and Lark. The dangers I've put in your path. I don't want anything to happen to any of you, and I fear that if something did, I wouldn't be able to forgive myself because it was my choice to leave."

Cora finally paused and looked at the headmistress. "We could have said no."

"Did you want to?"

Cora shook her head. "No. I wanted to come."

"So, you don't regret it?"

"No, I don't."

"Well, I'm relieved to hear that. You don't know how much

I've worried that you or any of the other women have regretted coming and have hated it."

"I could have done without the snake, but that is my only complaint."

"I could have done without the snake too. And the measles outbreak." Winona laughed, and although she'd dealt with one of her concerns, another weighed on her mind. "So . . . Mr. Scott seems like a nice young man."

"Yes, he is."

"And so does Mr. Wright."

"Yes, he is too."

Winona looked at Cora expectantly, waiting for her to continue. She didn't.

"I get the feeling that I was right in thinking that both men are interested in you, and I was wondering where your heart lay."

Cora's smile faltered slightly. "I'm not sure," she admitted. "I like them both, but I don't know which one I should choose."

Winona nodded understandingly. "What about them do you like?"

"They are both kind, and they want to make something of themselves in this world. Sometimes I fear what plans Jasper has—going to California and gold mining. I'm not sure I want to be the wife of a miner. Not to mention, I'm not sure I want to live in California."

"Perhaps he would change his mind if you asked, and you two could continue to Oregon as you planned."

"I don't know that he would wish to do that. It's his dream—gold and California."

"And what about Mr. Wright?"

"Sam would marry me tomorrow if I asked him to. Not that I want to be the one to ask. I want him to do the asking."

"Why do you hesitate then?"

"I don't know."

"May I speak freely?"

Cora's brow furrowed. "Of course."

Winona ignored Cora's suspicious tone. She wasn't trying to hide anything. It would all come out in just mere moments. "I like Mr. Scott. He's a good man, and he seems like he would make a fine husband."

"It sounds as though you are about to give me a but."

"No. I'm not. I like Mr. Scott."

"So, where does the hesitation come in?" Cora lifted her finger, circling it in the air.

"I'm not sure I can say the same about Mr. Wright. I don't know what it is, but there is something off about him."

Cora's expression changed. Her brow furrowed again, and she straightened her shoulders. "But I like Mr. Wright," she said. "He's kind to me, and he has good intentions."

"Are you sure about that?"

"Why do you ask?"

"I was putting away the blankets last night, and I overheard you two talking. I couldn't hear his exact words, but I could hear his tone. He was angry."

"At Mr. Scott. Not at me. Honestly, Winona, I think you are being far too concerned for nothing. I don't see anything wrong with him."

Winona sighed. She had seen this conversation going better in her head, yet she also knew she wasn't saying everything how she wanted. Everything was coming out wrong. "Cora, I'm not saying he's a bad man. I just don't want to see you get hurt."

"So you think he will hurt me?"

"No. That's not what I meant."

"Then what did you mean?"

"I don't know. There's something about Sam that I can't put my finger on, but it doesn't sit right with me."

"Well, I don't see what you see."

"And that's all right. Just please be careful."

Cora's eyes narrowed, and she looked hurt. "I don't need you to tell me who I should or shouldn't like, Winona," she said. "I'm perfectly capable of making my own decisions." She stood and brushed the dirt from her skirt.

Winona shook her head. "Cora, wait. Don't leave. I'm sorry I upset you. I didn't mean to. I just want what's best for you. I care about you, and I don't want to see you get hurt."

"Well, I won't get hurt. I'll be fine. And I'll make the choice on my own."

Cora grabbed the bucket's handle and turned. The bucket swung with her haste, and water splashed along the sandy beach.

"Cora, wait."

Winona stood and rushed a few steps after the young woman. Her heart sank at the thought of the damage she'd done. She knew she couldn't force Cora to choose one man over the other, no matter how much she wanted to protect her. All she could do was offer her advice and support and hope that Cora would make the right decision.

She turned away from watching the young woman leave and sat back in the sand. With a heavy sigh, she grabbed her bucket and rinsed off the last of the dishes.

~

CORA

Cora didn't look back as she walked away. Anger and hurt boiled inside her, making her feel like she could explode any minute. She couldn't believe Winona had the nerve to tell her whom she should like. As if she had any right to dictate who Cora could or couldn't be interested in.

I'm a grown woman, she thought. *I can do as I please.*

She continued back to the wagons stomping through the

grass with a huff to her breath. The bucket handle slipped out of her palm, landing on the ground with a thud, and as she bent down to pick it up, she heard a noise in the trees. The sound of a loud grunt and the faint sound of someone crying caused a lump in her throat.

She glanced over her shoulder. No one was around.

More grunts echoed, and as soon as they started, they stopped, and she heard footsteps running in the opposite direction.

"Hello?" she said. She didn't know why she did. It only would have scared her more if someone had answered. She crept into the trees, looking around the trunks for the source of the noise. Her heart raced. She had no idea what she would find, but a feeling of dread was growing in the pit of her stomach.

She took a step, tripping over a log or branch, and when she looked down to locate the chunk of wood, her gaze found something else instead—Mrs. Fairchild lying dead on the ground. The woman's lifeless eyes stared at the sky above them, and her clothes were ripped and tattered like someone had fought with her before killing her. She had red marks around her neck and had been strangled.

Cora screamed out in horror, and it echoed through the trees.

TEN

JASPER

No one ever knows what a dead body looks like until they see it, and while Jasper had seen his fair share of animals who had passed away, looking down at Mrs. Fairchild had been the first human. If he was honest with himself, he hoped that his first would also be his last too.

Jasper didn't know what had been the worst moment of this morning—hearing Cora's scream across the campsite, seeing her hysterical after he arrived to help her, or having to watch as Mr. Fairchild knelt over his dead wife, shouting as he asked anyone who would listen to him what happened and who killed his wife. While the men stood near the scene, the women stayed off in the distance; some even stayed at the wagons with the children.

"I want to know who did this!" Mr. Fairchild shouted with his gasped breaths. Tears streamed down his cheeks, and he cradled his wife in his lap. "Who did this?" He looked at Mr. Mills, who looked around at all the men, studying each of them as though he suspected everyone. "God, please don't take her. Please don't take her. Give her back to me!"

Jasper looked at Dr. Evans and Mr. Campbell, the blacksmith who stood on either side of him, and they looked at him, both shrugging their shoulder. Surely, neither of them would do such a thing. Well, the doctor, certainly. A newlywed with everything to lose, there wouldn't be a chance he could have done something like this. Jasper didn't know much about Mr. Campbell, but from the little dealings he had with the man, he thought of him as more of a shy and quiet type who didn't get his feathers ruffled easily. Jasper looked around at the other men. None of them, not even the cowboys who always had a gruffness to them, stood out to be that kind of man.

Who on earth would attack and kill a defenseless woman?

While Mr. Fairchild continued to beg and bargain with the Lord for his wife back, Mr. Mills moved toward Dr. Evans, and turning away from the crowd, he leaned in, whispering just loud enough that Jasper could hear the whole conversation. "Are you sure she was strangled?"

"There is no doubt in my mind. She has bruises around her neck, and there are no other injuries."

"She couldn't have fallen and snapped her neck?"

"Fallen on what? There is no cliff or ravine. Just falling from a standing position wouldn't have broken anything."

Mr. Mills sighed heavily. "I suppose we need to investigate this thoroughly. I want everyone to stay put until we figure this out."

"Mr. Mills, if I may speak?"

"Go ahead."

"What if it wasn't anyone on the wagon train? What if it was Indian?"

"They wouldn't just attack one woman and leave. All the warriors would come for a fight, and the men would be their first targets."

"What if it was just one, and he happened upon Mrs. Fairchild and thought she would alert the men at the camp..."

Mr. Mills shook his head. "I don't know. It doesn't sound like any Indian attack I've ever been through or heard about. Not to mention, I know most of the tribes in the area. They are peaceful people who trade with wagon trains. I don't see any of them doing this."

"That doesn't mean it can't happen."

"You're right. But still. I don't know if I should hang my hat on such a theory."

"If you don't, you're looking at the prospect of accusing every man on this wagon train." As soon as Dr. Evans said the words, he and the wagon master looked around at the crowd.

Just as the two men looked around, so did Jasper, and he stopped on every single man. Mr. Reed, Mr. Stonemill, Mr. Collins, Mr. Dunning, and the German husband who he wasn't sure of his name—they all stared at the grisly scene with utter horror and sadness for Mr. Fairchild as though husband to husband; they understood his pain more than the few single men—Mr. Stanley, Mr. Bushman, and the cowboys—could understand.

Low murmurs of conversation hummed through the travelers, and Jasper noticed that some of them were looking at each other suspiciously as if trying to read guilt in each other's faces. He didn't blame them—the situation was tense and tragic, and it was only natural to look for someone to blame.

"You're right. It's a nightmare to think about, having to question and suspect all these men. But if I blame an Indian scout and I'm wrong..."

Dr. Evans rubbed his forehead and closed his eyes. A hint of frustration warmed through his exhaled breath. "I know. I know. If we don't find out who did this, we've just allowed a killer to stay amongst all the other women on this wagon train."

Jasper's stomach twisted.

Cora.

What if she was next? He couldn't let that happen. He had to do something. He wasn't about to stand by and allow someone to stay in the wagon train who would hurt any woman—most of all her.

He glanced around. *Where was she?*

"Who found Mrs. Fairchild again?" the wagon master asked.

"Miss Randall. She's one of the young women traveling with Miss Callahan."

Mr. Mills rolled his eyes. "Miss Callahan. Of course, this would involve her. Where is Miss Randall?"

"She's with the women." Dr. Evans pointed in another direction, and before he could finish his sentence, Mr. Mills took off and headed for where the women were gathered. Dr. Evans followed, and as Jasper darted after the two of them, the doctor glanced over his shoulder and stopped. He raised an eyebrow. "Mr. Scott?"

"I'd like to help," Jasper said.

"I'm not sure that's a good idea."

"Please. I have a . . . *vested interest* in Miss Randall. I was also the first one to find her crying. I heard her scream from my wagon."

Dr. Evans looked at Mr. Mills, who nodded. "He couldn't have done it. I saw him at his wagon, tending to his laundry all morning."

Dr. Evans glanced down to the ground as a slight smile inched across his lips for a second. He looked back up at Jasper. "Ah. I see. Well, come on."

The three men made their way over to where the women were standing. Cora was in the middle, with Miss Callahan and the other women she traveled with huddled around her. Mr. Wright lurked in the back, and he shot Jasper a glare as he approached.

"Cora?" Dr. Evans said. "Mr. Mills would like to ask you a few questions."

Cora wiped the tears streaming down her face, and she gave Miss Callahan a fleeting look before turning to Mr. Mills and nodding.

"Um. All right." Cora's shoulders tightened. She inched closer, her feet barely making contact with the ground as if she was trying to make herself as small as possible. Her hands were now clasped in front of her, and her fingers nervously fidgeted. She looked as though she wanted to melt into the ground and disappear, never to be seen again.

Jasper fought the urge to wrap his arms around her. He wanted to grab her and hold onto her, never letting go for as long as he lived. He wanted to protect her from all the evil the world wanted to throw at her.

"Can you tell me what happened?" Mr. Mills asked her.

Cora glanced up at him, her eyes wide with fear before she quickly broke away and stared at her feet instead. "Yes sir," she said softly before adding, "Winona and I were washing dishes in the river, and I decided to return to the wagon."

"You left alone?"

"Yes, sir. We were . . . talking, and I didn't want to hear what she was saying, so I got frustrated, and I left. I was walking toward the camp when I heard odd noises coming from the trees."

"What noises?"

"Grunts and faint cries."

"Would you say it sounded like someone was strangling someone else?"

She closed her eyes, and more tears streamed down her cheeks. "Is that what happened to Mrs. Fairchild?" she whispered in a small voice.

"I'm afraid it was. So, would you say that is the sound you heard?"

"Um. I don't know. I suppose so. I've never heard someone

strangle someone before . . ." Her voice trailed off, and she bit her lip nervously.

"Of course, you haven't. That's not what I meant. Did you see anyone in the trees or while walking around?"

She shook her head. "No. I didn't see anyone other than Mrs. Fairchild." She closed her eyes again and wrapped her arms around her shoulders, hugging herself. Her body trembled.

"Perhaps we should give her a minute," Jasper suggested to the other two men.

Mr. Mills glanced at him, narrowing his eyes for a second, then nodding. "You're probably right." The wagon master backed away from Cora, Dr. Evans, and Jasper. He turned and walked a few steps toward another tree, and without another word, he rested his arm on the trunk, blowing out a deep breath.

Jasper reached out, rubbing Cora's arm. "I'm sorry you have to deal with this," he said.

Her eyes were swollen and bloodshot, and they welled with tears as she looked at him. His heart sank. She opened her mouth to speak, but before she could say anything, Sam slithered up beside her, laying his hands on her shoulders.

"I believe I told you to stay away from her," Sam said to Jasper. His jaw clenched, and he hissed his words.

Jasper's eyes narrowed, and he opened his mouth. Before he could say a word, though, he heard Mr. Mills clear his throat behind him. The subtle warning told Jasper he should be quiet.

"Do we have a problem, Mr. Wright?" the wagon master asked.

Sam looked from Jasper to Mr. Mills. The tension in his shoulders softened, but only a little, as though he was forced to calm down, not because he wanted to. He shook his head. "No, sir."

"Good. I don't need anything else happening right now. Not

when we have a dead woman and a husband in mourning. I don't need two grown men fighting for one reason or another." He had a slight growl to his voice, and Jasper dropped his gaze to the ground. Guilt prickled in his chest. Mr. Mills was right. No matter how he felt about Sam right now, it didn't matter over the murder and loss of Mrs. Fairchild. Helping to find who had killed the woman should—and would—be his priority.

"Everyone should go back to their wagons. I'll be around to talk to everyone and ask questions about where you all were this morning after I get Mr. Fairchild settled. We will stay camped here for the day. Perhaps longer." Mr. Mills rubbed his chin, and his eyes looked around at all the women. "For now, keep close to your wagons. If you need to go to the river, let me know." He turned to leave, then paused and glanced over his shoulder. "Dr. Evans. Mr. Scott. Will you two come with me?"

Dr. Evans nodded, hesitating for a moment while he reached for his wife. He kissed and hugged her before telling her to stay with Miss Callahan and that he would return as soon as he could. She wiped her tear-stained cheeks and nodded.

As Jasper turned to follow the wagon master, Miss Callahan stepped forward, reaching for his arm. "Mr. Scott?"

"Yes, ma'am."

"I was wondering if—when you are finished with whatever Mr. Mills needs of you—if you could stay close to my wagon. I'm traveling alone with three young women, and . . . we have no male companions other than Dr. Evans, who has his own responsibilities . . ." She dropped her gaze and then looked back at him. Her eyes were puffy and red from crying, and he could feel the fear in her body.

"Of course, I will help you in any way I can, and I will move my wagon next to yours as soon as I'm finished. You don't have to worry."

"Thank you."

Although Jasper heard Sam growl, he ignored the man, not even looking in Sam's direction. What Sam wanted didn't matter. If Miss Callahan asked him to help, he would help, and if Sam had a problem with it, he could drown himself in the river for all Jasper cared.

ELEVEN

JASPER

The fire cracked and popped as the flames charred the chunk of wood Dr. Evans placed in the middle. Jasper, the doctor, Sam, and all five women sat around, watching the bright glow with bowls of stew in their laps. None of them said a word. None of them even moved.

Mr. Mills had spent the whole afternoon talking to everyone on the wagon train, and he was nowhere nearer finding out what had happened to Mrs. Fairchild than he was when they had first found the body.

As the silence hung heavy in the air, Jasper felt a sense of unease in his stomach. He had seen death before, but the murder of Mrs. Fairchild had shaken him to the core. He glanced over at Dr. Evans, hoping for some reassurance, but the man stared into the flames with a distant look in his eyes. His arm was wrapped around his wife in a tight grip, and she had an equally far-off look about her.

Jasper cleared his throat, hoping to break the silence. "Have you thought about what you think happened to Mrs. Fairchild?" he asked.

The doctor looked up; his eyes were filled with sadness, yet

Jasper could see a hint of frustration in them. Only a fool wouldn't know that Dr. Evans was thinking that it was probably the same thing weighing on Jasper's mind too.

"I'm afraid I haven't," the doctor said. "There is nothing to go on, really. No one saw anything. Mr. Fairchild said she had gone down to the river for water. He didn't think much of it until he heard Cora scream, and someone told him about his wife." The doctor shook his head, blowing a breath as he squeezed his wife's shoulders harder. "I can't imagine what he's feeling right now."

His wife closed her eyes and tucked her chin to her chest.

Jasper nodded, feeling a wave of frustration wash over him as well. He had hoped the doctor could shed some light on the situation. "So, what do we do now?" he asked. "We can't just sit here and wait for the killer to strike again."

Dr. Evans let out a deep sigh. "You're right. We can't. We need to find out who did it, but it won't be easy, and walking around camp looking at everyone differently poses its own difficulties. We are supposed to trust one another on this wagon train. Are we not supposed to do that anymore?" Dr. Evans raised one eyebrow, cocking his head to the side. "Seems crazy to think about."

Jasper glanced over at Sam, sitting across the fire near Cora. Firelight blazed in his eyes, and although everyone around him looked broken and beaten down, as though they'd lost everything in the world, Sam didn't. Instead, he looked unphased by everything that was going on around him.

"We should search where Mrs. Fairchild was found for clues," Jasper said. He stared at Mr. Wright. "We might find something like ripped fabric or footprints—anything we can find that might lead us in the right direction."

The doctor's eyes narrowed. "We did a little, but we could again. I think Mr. Mills was trying to handle Mr. Fairchild more than anything this afternoon. He did talk to several of the men, though, asking them questions. Everyone he has spoken with has an alibi. He wants to talk to them again, though, and the ones I didn't speak to today."

"Is there anyone he hasn't talked to yet?" Although Jasper asked the doctor, he continued keeping his gaze on Mr. Wright. "Or anyone he suspects?"

"I don't know. He hasn't said so."

"Do you really think it was someone on this wagon train?" Miss McCall asked. A large crease formed on her forehead, and as she spoke, she grabbed Miss Linwell's hand, who was sitting beside her.

"I don't know how to answer that, Harper," Dr. Evans said. "All I can tell you is that you have to be careful. There could very well be a killer, who could be anyone, on this wagon train."

Both the two young women gasped and looked at each other.

"I think it's time for you ladies to turn in for the night and get some rest." Miss Callahan stood and made her way over to them, taking their bowls from their hands. She leaned down, kissing the tops of both of their heads before turning to Cora and laying her hand on Cora's shoulder. Cora flinched as though she hadn't taken much notice of anything that had been happening around her. "You should try to get some rest too."

Cora looked up at her headmistress. She opened her mouth as though she was going to protest but didn't, and she nodded, rising to her feet. Both Jasper and Sam stood, too, and while Jasper ignored Sam, Sam shot Jasper a glare.

Miss Callahan hugged all three women before watching the three make their way to the wagon and climb inside. Jasper watched them, too, fighting against the urge to follow them to ensure they were safe and sound. Doing so would only scare them even more, and with the wagon being mere feet from the campfire, it was pointless. There was nothing he could do now but wait until morning when they could continue searching for Mrs. Fairchild's killer.

Once the women had disappeared into the safety of the back of the wagon, Miss Callahan folded her arms across her chest and heaved a deep sigh as she walked back to the fire. Her steps were heavy with sorrow, and she stopped when she reached Dr. Evans. "We must find who did this before it happens again, Carter."

"I agree." Dr. Evans glanced between those left sitting around the fire before turning to his wife. "Are you ready to head back to our wagon?"

She shook her head. "No. Not yet." Her gaze fluttered toward Sam, who had taken his seat across the fire. Anger seemed to seethe through her.

"Did Mr. Mills tell you anything, Carter?" Miss Callahan asked. Whether she noticed Mrs. Evans as Jasper had, he didn't know, but she didn't act as though she did. "Does he have any idea who it could have been?"

"He didn't say. But I'm sure we will catch whoever did this, Winona," the doctor said firmly. "I know it's hard, but the important thing right now is not to worry, or at least don't worry too much. We will find out what happened."

"How do you know?"

"It usually is only a matter of time before we find something that will lead us to the murderer, whether it's someone on the wagon train or perhaps an Indian who had come across Mrs. Fairchild and killed her because they feared she would scream."

"You are asking the impossible in asking me not to worry. You know that, right?"

Dr. Evans nodded. "I do, and I'm sorry for it."

She chewed on her lip and then asked the doctor. "What do you think about the whole situation? Do you think it was an Indian? Or do you think it was someone on the wagon train? If it's the latter . . . do you have any idea who could have done this?"

Jasper snorted. "I do." The words left his lips before he even had the chance to think about uttering them. Truth be told, he hadn't had one particular person in mind, or at least he hadn't until now. The only reason he'd spoken was that when Miss Callahan had asked, Sam popped into his head, and he couldn't deny that a slight twinge of regret twisted in his stomach. It wasn't like him to accuse someone without evidence, and he had nothing to go on regarding proof.

Proof, he thought. *But did he have proof?*

Sam had already propositioned another man's wife. In fact, it was the married couple sitting just to Jasper's left. Had he tried to have his way with Mrs. Fairchild, and when she rebuffed him, he—fearing she would tell her husband—killed her to save himself?

"You know who it is?" Miss Callahan's mouth gaped open, and she brushed her fingers against her collarbone.

Jasper cleared his throat. "No. I . . . I shouldn't have said that. I just . . . thought of something, and I spoke without considering what I was saying. Forgive me, ma'am."

Dr. Evans whipped his head towards Jasper, flashing Jasper a slight look as though he knew what Jasper was thinking—or at least that was the impression Jasper got—before returning his gaze to Miss Callahan. "I don't know who could have done it, Winona, and I don't even have a clue," he said, his voice barely above a whisper.

"Who do you suspect?" Sam asked, pointing his chin toward Jasper. His voice was laced with a slight growl.

"I prefer not to say until I have more information."

"Figures."

The two men stared at one another, and Jasper's eye twitched. He couldn't help but take notice of the man, who had remained strangely silent throughout their conversation, with the exception of the last question he'd just asked Dr. Evans. He hadn't even said goodnight to Cora nor stood when she turned in. He'd just sat there the whole time, staring at Jasper.

"What do you think, Mr. Wright?" Jasper asked him. "Do you have any thoughts or opinions on the matter?"

Sam cleared his throat and shook his head slowly, looking down at the ground. "Nope. I don't have an idea or thoughts on the situation."

"Nothing at all? That's surprising. I would think you would have an opinion about it since you seem to have an opinion about everything. Especially when it comes to the likes of Miss Randall."

Sam clenched his jaw and shook his head again. He had an air about him. "I have nothing to say because I'm not the one who is always down at the river, panning for gold." His words were thick with the insinuation that Jasper almost knew was coming even before Sam opened his mouth to speak.

"You're right. You aren't always down by the river, panning for gold. But I am, or at least I usually am. I wasn't this morning."

"Can you prove it?"

"I can. Not only did I have a conversation with Mr. Stonemill and Mr. Reed, but I was talking to Mr. Mills when we heard Cora scream." Jasper cocked his head to the side. He never liked entertaining a condescending tone as he always felt men who did it were arrogant, but he almost reveled in it this time. "Can you say the same about yourself and where you were this morning when Mrs. Fairchild was killed?"

"I was out hunting this morning in the opposite direction."

"And did anyone see you leave or come back? Can anyone say you couldn't have possibly done it?"

Sam jumped to his feet, clenching one fist while he pointed at Jasper with the other hand. Jasper jumped up too, as did Dr. and Mrs. Evans, and while the doctor remained by Jasper's side, his wife moved toward Miss Callahan. The two women stared with wide eyes.

"How dare you accuse me. I was hunting. Period," Sam shouted.

"Oh, but it's fine if you accuse me?"

"I think you both should calm down." Dr. Evans moved between the two men, holding his arms up. "I know you two don't care for one another, but shouting at each other is not helping the situation."

"He shouldn't even be here," Sam said, pointing at Jasper again. "He needs to leave."

"I need to leave?" Jasper pressed his finger into his own chest, then returned the gesture, pointing at Sam. "I think it's you who needs to leave. No one sitting around this campfire wants you here. Miss Callahan asked me to join her tonight, and Dr. and Mrs. Evans . . . well, I'm quite shocked they want you here after what you did to her. I'm surprised Dr. Evans is even speaking to you. How did you spin that tale to fake your innocence?"

The doctor's head whipped toward Jasper. "What did you say?"

Sam's eyes widened, and he backed up a few steps, nearly tripping on the log he'd been sitting on.

"What did you say?" Dr. Evans asked again, turning his attention toward Jasper; he moved closer. "What did Sam do to my wife?"

Jasper's heart thumped. "I . . ." He looked at the doctor's wife. "I thought he would know."

She shook her head, and the look on her face was like a punch to Jasper's gut. He didn't want to tell another person's secrets or come between a husband and wife.

"I'm so sorry," he said to her.

Dr. Evans moved toward her. "What is he talking about?"

"It was nothing."

"Obviously, it wasn't."

She looked at Jasper and then at Sam. "Mr. Wright came to the wagon after you left. He . . . implied he could please me better than you." She bit her bottom lip and closed her eyes.

Dr. Evans didn't wait for her to say another word before spinning to face Sam. "Get away from here. Get away from my wife." The doctor lunged toward Sam, and Jasper caught him, holding him back. While Jasper wanted nothing more than to let the doctor rip into the very man Jasper hated more than anything, now wasn't the time. "You stay away from my wife. You stay away from Miss Callahan, Miss Linwell, and Miss McCall, and you, certainly, stay away from Miss Randall. If I see you around them again, I will kill you."

Sam took off, vanishing in the darkness while Dr. Evans, still struggling against Jasper's hold on him, repeated his threat.

Jasper glanced over as Cora came running from the back of the wagon. She skidded to a stop, looking at Miss Callahan, Mrs. Evans, Dr. Evans, and Jasper, and then toward the darkness where Sam had vanished.

"Where did Sam go?" she asked.

Dr. Evans finally wiggled from Jasper's grasp and yanked his shirt straight, "It doesn't matter. He's not welcome around any of you anymore."

TWELVE

CORA

Although Cora heard Carter's words, they hadn't registered in her mind. "What do you mean he's not... I don't understand." Cora rubbed her forehead. Her head pounded, and her breath quickened. She turned toward Winona. "What happened?"

Winona gulped a breath and made her way toward Cora, wrapping her arms around the young woman in a tight hug. "Everything is going to be all right."

"But what happened? I don't understand."

She pulled away from the headmistress as Harper and Grace ran from the wagon. They stopped, looking around at everyone. "What happened?" Harper asked.

"That's what I would like to know." Cora looked at Jasper, and when he wouldn't answer, she moved on to Carter. "Why isn't he allowed near us?"

"Because of what he did to Lark, my wife."

Cora's head not only pounded, but it started to spin. "I don't understand. What do you mean because of what he did to Lark?"

"Mr. Scott said that Mr. Wright went to my wagon looking

for me, and when he found out I wasn't there, he . . . bothered my wife."

"Bothered? As in how?" Although Cora asked Carter the question, she made a *pfft* sound and held up her hand. She moved away from him, heading toward Lark. "How did he *bother* you?"

Lark glanced up at the sky and blew out a breath. She fidgeted on her feet, rocking her weight from side to side. She looked as though she didn't want to answer the question any more than Cora wanted to ask it—or hear the answer. "He implied that somehow my past meant I didn't have a problem joining other men in bed even though I was married."

Cora snorted, shaking her head as she scrunched her face. "Sam isn't like that."

"Are you saying I'm lying?" Lark furrowed her brow, deepening her tone.

"I'm saying you might have misunderstood what he was trying to say. He wouldn't do as you said he did, and he's never acted indecently with me."

"Perhaps he thought he could because of Lark's past." Winona skirted around Cora, standing between the two women.

"You're taking her side?" Cora looked between the two women.

"That's not what I'm doing." The headmistress shook her head. "I'm only trying to give a different perspective."

"That's not a different perspective. And I don't know why you are saying anything at all. You've never liked him. I just don't think Lark understood what he was trying to say." Cora paused, her anger bubbling for the one woman who always seemed to be the root of the ruin in her life. Why was Lark always the cause of strife and trouble? "I don't believe you," Cora said to Lark, folding her arms across her chest.

Cora crossed her arms over her chest, her gaze meeting Lark's. "I don't believe you."

"Would you believe me?" Jasper moved toward the two. His shoulders were hunched, and he scratched the back of his neck as though doing so was supposed to convey his regret for speaking up. "Because it's true. I heard every word he said to her."

Cora's mind was racing as she tried to process the information. She couldn't believe that Sam, the man she thought she could love and thought she knew, would do something like this. She stared at Jasper, her mouth agape and her thoughts spinning. Her gaze shifted back to Lark.

Winona stepped forward, her voice low and calming. "Let's all just take a moment to breathe."

The tension in the air was thick as everyone nodded in agreement, though no one said anything out loud. Cora took a deep breath as Winona wrapped an arm around her shoulders and guided her away from the other women, giving them some space. Cora sighed, feeling defeated. She wanted so badly to believe that Sam couldn't act in such an indecent manner, but the evidence was stacking up against him--and it didn't look good for him at all.

Harper stepped forward and reached out, rubbing Cora's arm. Cora's mind was racing as she tried to process the information. She couldn't believe that Sam, the man she thought she could love and thought she knew, would do something like this. She looked at Jasper pleadingly, begging him with her eyes for him to tell her it wasn't true.

Cora shook her head in disbelief and folded her arms across her chest. Tears misted her eyes as she recalled the conversations they had shared. Why had he even talked to her if his interest lay elsewhere? What was the point of it all? "That doesn't make any sense. "Why? Why would he do something like this?" Cora asked softly.

Carter moved over to Lark. "Why didn't you tell me?"

"Because I didn't want it to cause any strife on the trip. I just want to get to Oregon and start our lives."

"You still should have told me."

"I know."

Cora watched as the husband and wife embraced. A flicker of anger sparked in her chest. Once again, she was alone without anyone to call her own, and Lark had something to do in sealing the fate—whether she had meant to or not. What did it matter if she hurt Lark? She could return to her handsome husband whenever she wanted.

While Cora had no one.

The spark of anger grew.

She wanted answers. She wanted to know why.

She spun on her heel and darted off.

"Cora? Where are you going?"

Although Cora heard Jasper and Winona calling her name as they followed her, she didn't stop.

∾

The night air was thick and oppressive, and Cora stumbled through the darkness, her fear and anger fueling her even though she couldn't see more than a few feet in front of her. She tripped several times, hitting the ground with her knees and hands. She winced as the rocks scuffed her palms and the wounds stung. She didn't care, though. All she cared about was getting to Sam. She wanted to know the truth, from him, about what happened with Lark.

She continued through the darkness, managing as best as she could from the moonlight and the little light the campfires gave off until she finally reached Sam's wagon. She could see him tacking up one of his wagon horses, and she ran toward him, slamming her body into his. He was like a wall, and she bounced back, nearly losing her balance.

He whirled around, bracing his whole body. "What are you doing here?" He asked incredulously.

She looked at his face in the faint light of the campfire, and as she moved toward him, his eyes widened with surprise and something else she couldn't put her finger on. Fear? Guilt? Cora couldn't quite tell what it was.

"Is it true?" she said, keeping her voice calm and low. "Is it true what you did to Lark?"

His brow furrowed. "I don't have to answer to you or anyone."

"You're right; you don't have to. But I would think you would want to. I would think you would want to tell me what happened."

"I don't want to tell you anything."

Cora took a deep breath and stepped back, shaking her head. Clearly, he wouldn't say anything more about it, and her anger now boiled in her veins. She couldn't take it anymore. She lunged toward him, clenching her fists and pounding them on his chest as she continued to scream the question.

He shifted his weight, grabbing her by the wrists and spinning her around. He slammed her up against the side of the wagon. The wheel dug into her back, shooting pain throughout her entire body. She could feel his hot breath on her skin and the hatred in his eyes.

Her anger turned into fear.

"How dare you touch me," he said. With one hand still gripped on her wrist, he took the other hand and clenched her neck, squeezing against her throat. She ripped at his arm, trying to make him loosen his tight hold. He didn't, and he squeezed even harder. She couldn't breathe. "I don't want to hurt you, but I will. I've done it before, and I will do it again if I have to."

"Let go of me," she begged through gasps as she tried to claw and kick her way free.

"I can't believe you are making me do this," he said. "I loved you, and now you're making me hurt you. I don't want to."

"Then don't."

"I can't stop now. You know the truth. It's dangerous for you to know the truth." His eyes traced all along her face. "I don't want you to end up like her. Like the other one."

"What other one?" Cora's blood ran cold, and she gasped. "It was you," she whispered. "You strangled Mrs. Fairchild."

He held on tighter and tighter. Her vision blurred, and her lungs begged for breath. Sam opened his mouth, but before he could say a word, another body collided with his from the side. His grip still held onto her, and the force jerked her to the ground. The force of the impact knocked the breath out of her, and she lay there, gasping for air. He released his grip and grabbed Jasper, who had attacked him from the side. The two men wrestled on the ground, rolling and punching each other as they struggled. They both grunted.

Jasper pinned Sam to the ground with his knees as he rained blows down upon him. Sam writhed and twisted, throwing punches as he struggled and clawed out from under Jasper. He scrambled to his feet and ducked, dodging one vicious blow after another. Jasper lunged for him again with a furious barrage of punches. Sam ducked and weaved, evading Jasper's swinging arms, until finally, he shifted and landed a solid blow to Jasper's jaw.

Cora screamed as Jasper staggered backward. He shook his head as though it rang, and Sam moved toward him, throwing another few punches at Jasper's face.

Cora turned away from the men, hiding her face behind her hands. She feared the outcome.

A gunshot rang through the air, and she screamed, flinging herself back.

"Cora! Cora!" Winona's voice shouted through the air, and as Cora opened her eyes, her headmistress dropped to her knees, wrapping her arms around the young woman. She looked over as Mr. Mills ran for the two men. Just before the wagon master reached them, Sam shoved Jasper off him and darted for the horse. He reached the animal before Jasper or Mr. Mills could grab him, and he climbed into the saddle, spurring the horse into a dead run away from the camp.

Jasper struggled to his feet and wiped the blood trickling down his chin.

"Are you all right?" Mr. Mills asked him.

He nodded, then turned and stumbled to Cora and Winona. He fell mere feet from them, and the two women crawled to him. His lungs heaved, and blood streamed from cuts on his head. Winona ripped some material from her skirt and pressed it against the wounds. He winced.

"Are . . . are you all right?" he asked Cora. His voice was strained.

"Yes," she said. Tears filled her eyes and streamed down her cheeks.

THIRTEEN

JASPER

The endless expanse of grassland stretched out as far as the eye could see, broken only by the occasional rocky outcrop or the winding path of a shallow stream as Jasper stood upon a grassy plain.

The endless expanse stretched out around him like a sea of emerald and gold, and he felt the early morning rays upon his face, the chill of the air in his lungs, and the distant flutter of the breeze blowing across the land. A hawk circled above, looking down on the earth for its breakfast, and its caw echoed. Yet, despite all the signs of life and nature around him, an eerie stillness seemed to hang in the air. The sky was a brilliant shade of blue, dotted with fluffy white clouds. But there was a stillness in the air that made Jasper's skin crawl. Beautiful but eerie, it was as if the land itself was holding its breath, waiting for something to happen.

Perhaps it was Jasper who was waiting.

And it wasn't the land at all.

As he rode through the Nebraska plains, Jasper felt a sense of unease settle over him. He squinted into the hazy distance, trying to detect any signs of movement or life. He had never hunted another man before, nor had he ever thought he would. But here he was, riding through the rugged terrain, searching for a man who had committed a terrible crime. Sure, there were times when he was a young boy that he dreamed of being a Pinkerton, and he and his friends used to play games where one of them robbed a bank and went on the run while the others chased him down. But as he grew up, those games stopped. It wasn't that he didn't like the thought of working for the law or bringing criminals to justice; he just had too much farmer in him for anything else.

Jasper's horse trudged up the hill, breathing heavily as it crested the ravine and then headed downhill toward the river. The animal was tired, and so was Jasper. He had been riding since before dawn with the rest of the men on the wagon train, following the faint trail of the man they were hunting. They had lost the trail several times already, but each time someone had fortunately managed to pick it up again. They had to find Mr. Wright before he could do any more harm.

"The trail goes to the river but doesn't pick back up on the other side," Mr. Mills glanced at Jasper as he pulled his horse up alongside the wagon master and the wagon master's horse. Dr. Evans trotted up not long after, along with Mr. Campbell, the blacksmith.

"Mr. Stonemill, Mr. Reed, Mr. Stanley, and Mr. Bushman said they would head East for a bit and see what they can find. Mr. Collins, Mr. Stanley, Mr. Dunning, and the cowboys, Willy and Ernst, went West. They will shoot a couple of rounds in the air if they see Mr. Wright," Dr. Evans said.

"Which is both a good and bad idea." Mr. Mills let out a groan, shaking his head.

"Why?"

"Well, sure, it alarms us to any news that they have found

him, but it also lets him know." Mr. Mills yanked a handkerchief from his pocket and wiped his face. "They aren't going to find him anyway."

"Why not?"

"He's traveling in the river. But, as I told Mr. Scott, the problem is I don't know which direction he's headed."

"And I still don't know what that means." Jasper glanced in both directions.

"It means he's traveling either upriver or downriver, using the water to hide which direction."

"Surely, he's going to go back to Fort Kearney. If he continued to Fort Laramie, then either we would catch up to him or meet at the Fort." Mr. Campbell chuckled and then adjusted his seat on his horse.

The blacksmith had a point, Jasper thought. It would be stupid for Mr. Wright to continue on a trail where there was a chance the wagon train would catch up to him.

"What do we do now?" Jasper asked.

"Well, that's the crux of it. If we head back to Fort Kearney, we risk running out of cattle and supplies before reaching Oregon."

"Can't we buy more? We still have Fort Hall and Fort Boise ahead of us."

Mr. Mills shook his head. "It's not that simple."

"So, it sounds like you're saying we continue West."

"We have to."

Dr. Evans adjusted his hat and looked out across the river. "What do we tell Mr. Fairchild, then? You know he will want us to continue looking for Mr. Wright at all costs."

"And I would love to do that too. But I've got a job to do, Doctor. I've got to get the rest of these people, you and your wife included, to Oregon. I can't expect to go after a man who could be anywhere in the country in a matter of weeks with a wagon train full of families. If he wants to go after Mr. Wright himself, he can. I ain't stopping him. But it would be better for him to continue to Fort Hall, where he can send a telegram to all the nearby law and see if he can't get a Pinkerton on the case. That's his best option. I ain't the law. Neither are you, Mr. Campbell, Mr. Scott, or any other man on this wagon train."

All the men around the wagon master looked at one another. While part of Jasper disagreed, he also couldn't help but see the man's point. He wasn't the law. Nor did he have the right to take a man's punishment into his own hands. No matter how he felt, unless Mr. Wright returned and threatened another woman's life on the wagon train, his fate and punishment for his crimes would have to be carried out by a Pinkerton and a judge. Not a farmer from Missouri.

"Well, I guess we've done all we can this morning. We should head back to the wagons. We've got a funeral, and Lord only knows what else we will find when we return."

The group continued in silence, the only sound of the rustling of leaves and the crunching of horses' hooves on the forest floor.

~

WESTON

In all the years.
Of all the wagon trains.

And all the times Weston had taken this bloody trail, he'd never had a murder.

The wagon master glanced up at the sky, shaking his head. *Why now, God,* he thought.

This particular trip had to be cursed, and the problem was that he didn't know why. He'd always tried to do what was best by people. He never overcharged them. He always made sure everyone had the supplies they needed and that they were safe. He'd even gone against his better judgment and let that Miss Callahan and the four young women on the wagon train, for Pete's sake, which he hadn't exactly wanted to do, but after he saw the desperation behind her eyes—even if she tried to hide it—he felt bad.

What was it about this trip that would give him such bad luck?

A slight groan left his lips as he cued his horse back toward camp. The rest of the men rode staggered behind him. He didn't like the thought of what he would have to say to Mr. Fairchild when they returned, but there was nothing he could do. He couldn't change what happened any more than he could change the fact that they hadn't been able to find Mr. Wright.

He had known they wouldn't when they left camp this morning, but just because he knew it and could tell Mr. Fairchild, it didn't mean the husband would listen.

Not that Weston blamed the man.

He'd lost his wife. Nothing about that fact would make a man reasonable or think clearly.

The men continued back to the camp, and as they approached, the wives and children came out to greet them. They all lifted their hands to their faces to shield the sun's bright glare.

Mr. Fairchild ran toward them, and as he reached them, he bent over, catching his breath.

"Any sign of him?" he asked through his gasps. The man's face was etched with worry and grief, and Weston couldn't help but feel a twinge of sympathy for him.

Weston grimaced as he swung one leg over the saddle and dismounted his horse. He made his way over to the man, laying his hand on Mr. Fairchild's shoulder. He shook his head, and upon hearing the news, Mr. Fairchild sobbed.

Weston cleared his throat before speaking, "I'm sorry we weren't able to find him," he said softly.

Mr. Fairchild's gaze snapped up to meet Weston's, his eyes full of anger and sorrow, and his face crumpled in agony. He opened his mouth to say something, but no words came out. Instead, he just shook his head and looked off into the distance with his shoulders slumped in defeat.

Weston sighed quietly before continuing, "We followed his tracks for as long as we could, but he vanished in the river." His voice grew softer as he spoke, knowing that what he said wouldn't make Mr. Fairchild feel better about the situation. All they could do now was hope they would somehow find Mr. Wright and Mr. Fairchild would get his justice.

Mr. Fairchild nodded slightly before finally turning back toward Weston with a resigned expression, "Thank you for trying," he murmured before walking back into his wagon without another word.

"We will help with the funeral. I'll have the men dig the hole so you don't have to."

"Thank you for the offer, but I think I'd like to do it alone."

Weston nodded and watched as Mr. Fairchild disappeared into his wagon. A spark of anger hinted deep in his chest. This was not the way he had wanted this trip to go. Not in the slightest.

We aren't even halfway to Oregon yet, he thought. *What else was going to happen?*

~

"It is with great sadness that we gather today to say goodbye to a lovely woman. A woman who was taken from her husband far too soon by an evil in this world which we all fight against every day."

As Preacher Levinson continued to begin his sermon for

Mrs. Fairchild's funeral, Weston couldn't help but slightly—and silently—snort at the preacher's words. There were many evils in this world, and for some reason, he couldn't shake the feeling that they were all about to happen to this wagon train.

"But we shall take comfort in the fact that God is with us just as He is now with Mrs. Fairchild. In the short time that I have known her and her husband, I have come to know them as good, hardworking people. They brought joy to those around them, and Mrs. Fairchild will be missed, and our journey will never be the same without her. As we lay her to rest today, let us remember her kind spirit. Let us remember her infectious laughter, her quick wit, and her generous heart. Let us honor her memory by carrying on the journey she started and by always striving to be the best versions of ourselves. Let us pray."

Everyone bowed their heads.

"Dear Lord, we ask that You take Mrs. Fairchild into Your loving arms and welcome her into Heaven. We also ask that You look over her husband, comforting him in his time of sorrow and need. We know nothing will replace her love in his life, but we pray he finds the peace he needs in You. And it is with this that we pray in Jesus' name. Amen."

"Amen."

As the crowd dispersed, making their way back to their wagons, Weston stayed near the grave with Mr. Fairchild, who had remained kneeling by the mound of dirt, sobbing.

Ernst and Willy, the two cowboys, rode up, and as Weston turned to face them, they both removed their hats and nodded. Their horses shook their heads and swished their tails, fighting off the flies that annoyed them.

"We just wanted to know what the plan was, boss," Ernst said. He moved the reed of grass he'd been chewing on from one side of his mouth to the other, and the blade flapped with the movement.

"We will head out in the morning. Do you have all the cows rounded up?"

"Yes, sir. They are grazing around the river."

"Good. Try to keep them there until morning."

"What are you going to do about Mr. Wright's belongings?"

"We will keep the horses and the supplies." Weston glanced at the husband, still mourning his dead wife. "And I'll give them to Mr. Fairchild if he wants them. If he doesn't, I'll ask around and see if any of the other families want them."

"And the wagon?"

"Just leave it unless someone wants it. But I've got no use for it. It would probably be good to take the wheels but leave the rest."

"Do you think Mr. Wright will come back for his things?" Willy asked.

"Not unless he's a fool. But then again, he hasn't made the best choices so far, so who knows. Do you still have Mr. Stanley riding with you to help with the cows?"

"Yes, sir." Ernst moved the blade of grass again, shifting it from one side of his mouth to the other.

"Good. Keep him on the livestock as much as you can. I'd rather have three of you with them than just two."

The two cowboys nodded, cued their horses, and rode back toward the river. Weston placed his hat back on his head, squinting as he looked around the camp. He didn't want to think that Mr. Wright would try to come for anything or anyone, but he also didn't want to be the unprepared fool either.

A slight groan vibrated through his chest as he made his way over to Mr. Fairchild and removed his hat. "Mr. Fairchild, I wanted to extend my deepest condolences again."

Mr. Fairchild looked up with his tear-streaked face and nodded.

"I apologize if this may offend you, but we need to head out in the morning."

"I understand." The man's voice was barely a whisper.

"I'm giving you Mr. Wright's horses and supplies if you want them. I know it's not much, and it certainly doesn't compensate for your loss."

"No, it doesn't. But thank you."

"You're welcome. I'll leave you to your thoughts." Weston walked off without another word, leaving the poor man to sob for his wife again. He didn't want to look over his shoulder, but as he did, he saw Mr. Fairchild lying in the dirt next to the grave.

Weston continued toward his wagon, and as he neared it, Miss Callahan stood from sitting by his campfire. Another groan vibrated through his chest.

And just what does this woman want, he wondered.

"Good afternoon, Miss Callahan," he said, walking up to her. He tipped his hat before moving over to his water bucket, reaching for the ladle, and taking a much-needed drink.

"Good afternoon."

"What can I do for you?" While he had to ask, it didn't mean he wanted to.

"I spoke to Carter, and he mentioned that there will not be a search for Mr. Wright."

"That's right. I'm not the law, Miss Callahan. I have not jurisdiction to go after the man. Not to mention, my job is to get this wagon train to Oregon, and that's what I need to do."

"I understand. However, I'm concerned."

"About?"

"Mr. Wright knows where we are going and our pace. I'm concerned he will come for his supplies or . . . worse, come for someone he feels he has a claim to."

"I'm assuming you mean Miss Randall."

She dropped her gaze and then looked up at him again as she clasped her hands in front of her. Her fingers intertwined. "Yes. I am. I'm worried he will come back for her."

"I understand your concern, and I assure you I will do my best to protect everyone on this wagon train."

Her brow furrowed. "Are you sure?"

"I beg your pardon?"

"Well, you can't blame me for questioning your intentions or ability when you let Mr. Wright slip through your fingers the first time. Even after I came to you, asking about him. You didn't seem concerned about what I had approached you with, and now look what happened."

"Are you blaming me for Mrs. Fairchild's death?" The once hint of annoyance in his chest sparked into a small fire, and he grew even more tired of this conversation. Although he wasn't sure, he had an idea of what she was trying to say without actually saying the words, which made it even worse.

"No. I'm not, and that is not what I meant. However, I did come to you with concerns over Mr. Wright and . . . well . . . you ignored me."

There it was, he thought. *She was blaming him.*

He furrowed his brow and cleared his throat. "Are you saying you could have predicted what happened?"

"Again, no, that is not what I meant."

"But that is how it sounded. It sounds as though you thought something was odd with him, and had I looked into your *feelings*, I would have found the murderer that he was and somehow stopped it all from happening."

"That is not what I said. Don't put words in my mouth when I didn't say them."

"Well, if that wasn't what you said—in a roundabout manner—then what did you mean to say, Miss Callahan?"

She inhaled a deep breath and closed her eyes for a moment as she shook her head. "Never mind, Mr. Mills. Just forget I ever said anything. In fact, forget I ever came over this afternoon."

"Gladly."

Her mouth fell open, and she let out a scoffed *humphf* sound before stomping her foot and spinning on it. She strode away, swinging her arms with each step. He didn't know where on earth that woman got her gumption, but it was high time she left it behind before it got her into trouble.

If it hadn't already happened.

FOURTEEN

JASPER

Jasper sat at the helm of his wagon, the reins in his hands as he guided the horses across the rolling hills of the Wyoming prairie. The tall grass rippled in the gentle breeze, and he could see for miles in every direction. It was a vast, open land—one that he had always felt drawn to. There was something about the freedom of the prairie that called to him, that made him feel alive in a way that nothing else could.

Of course, with all of that, the sun was high in the sky, and its rays beat down on him, making the heat almost unbearable. If it wasn't for the view of the vast land around him, he might think it was some version of purgatory.

He snorted at that thought. Perhaps it already was.

They had been on the road for a few days since Mrs. Fairchild's murder, and each day there seemed to be a thicker and thicker blanket of tension that draped itself over the travelers on the wagon train. They had all been looking for a new start, a chance to make a life for themselves in the untamed wilderness of the West.

And what had they faced?

Disease.

Death.

Murder.

Jasper had little expectation for the trip when he left his parent's farm and arrived in Missouri. But the last thing he would have expected was what he'd lived through. In fact, if someone had told him he would face all he already had, he would have laughed and called the person an utter fool.

He thought of his parents and home for the first time in a while. He hadn't realized how much he missed it, but he did. Perhaps it was the sense of normalcy he missed. Certainly, there wouldn't have been a murder in Bell Buckle. It was too quiet, too perfect. In fact, Jasper couldn't think of a single crime committed in all the years he grew up there. Perhaps there might have been a time or two when a young boy grabbed an apple off a tree that wasn't his, but none of the farmers would have even cared out there. They probably would have grabbed a basket and filled it for the young lad, telling him to share it with his friends and family.

Man, Jasper loved that town.

But no matter how much he did, he also knew he needed something more in life. He wanted the mountains and streams of the untamed West. He wanted to hunt deer, see bears, and live in the wilderness where the wilds around him could kill him at any moment. He wanted the thrill of the unknown, and in the end, Bell Buckle would have suffocated him.

He snorted again. *Of course, the wilderness could kill him, so . . .*

The wagon in front of him stopped, and Jasper jerked his horses, telling them to whoa. They listened but threw their heads in the air as though to protest, even if it was just for a moment. Dust clouded around them, and Jasper jumped from the buckboard and made his way down the line.

He'd heard Mr. Mills talking about crossing the river today, but he didn't know where they would cross, and after passing the wagon in the front, he found the men standing near the riverbank, talking about how each wagon should cross.

"This one isn't as deep as the last, but everyone still needs to be careful," Mr. Mills told them. "We should stagger them a few feet apart so the wheels don't create ruts. It will make it harder for those at the end to push through."

"I know you want everyone in order, but you should let the German couple go first." Dr. Evans rested his hands on his hips. Although he spoke to Mr. Mills, he focused on the river. "I have a feeling the wife will have her baby soon, and I think it would give the husband some comfort if we were all able to help them."

"I understand, and you'll get no disagreement from me. Anyone else care to say no?" Mr. Mills looked around, and everyone standing with them shook their head. "I'll let them know. They don't speak much English, but I can help them understand." While Mr. Mills walked off to inform the German couple, Jasper studied the river. It was wider than the one they'd already crossed, and while it looked simple compared to the rapids he'd seen at times, he knew better than to blindly trust the water.

Water and wagons weren't friends.

Not in the slightest.

～

Jasper stood near the water's edge as the German couple guided their wagon toward the water. The husband's brow furrowed while the wife gripped the side of the buckboard. Her huge pregnant belly moved from side to side as the wagon rocked.

The horses continued forward, slow and sure, and as they entered the river and the water rose around the wheels, the current tugged on the wood and steel, and the horses threw their heads as the weight made their jobs harder.

Suddenly, a loud crack echoed, and the wagon jerked and jolted to the left, then the right, leaning to one side that looked like it would tip over with just enough pressure. The wife screamed and closed her eyes, bracing against the buckboard while the husband switched both reins to one hand and looked over the side.

Jasper darted toward the wagon, as did all the other men from the wagon train, and all of them shouted for the husband not to move an inch.

"It's stuck!" Dr. Evans shouted. "We're going to have to push it."

"But not too hard, or it will tip." Mr. Mills ran to the front, pointing toward the other side of the river. "One step at a time," he said to the husband, holding one finger in the air. "Do you understand? One time. One step. Just one. Stop. Then one more. Stop. Then one more. Understand?"

"*Eins!*" the husband shouted, holding up one finger, too. "*Eins.*"

"Yes. One."

"One," the husband repeated in English, which sounded to Jasper like he was saying won more than one the number.

The men all gathered around the back of the wagon. The wheel was stuck in the muddy bottom of the river between several large rocks, and as the men started trying to free it, they shouted to one another, their voices strained with the weight of the stones. With every stone they removed, the wagon would jerk, and in danger of tipping over, Jasper shouted for them to stop until they could move the horses a few steps.

He ran to the front, struggling through the water that went up to his knees as he rounded the horses and grabbed the reins.

"Let go of the reins," he shouted to the German husband.

"*Was? Willst du mich loslassen?*" the husband said,

Jasper tugged on the reins. "Let go!"

He didn't know if the husband truly understood the words or the motion, but he released the reins, and Jasper yanked on the leather straps until the horses took a step. The hitch pressed against their weight, tightening the rigging around their chests. They tried to step backward to release the pressure, but Jasper yanked them forward again.

As the horses moved, the men shifted a few more stones. The wheel lurched but still wasn't free. Jasper asked the horses to move again, and when the straps tightened around their chest a second time, they threw their heads. Neither of the animals were happy, and by the way they started dancing around, he could tell they were losing patience.

They took a step back, and although he gently asked them forward, they both bolted, slamming into the harness, which threw them both backward. After one panicked, the other did too, and the second reared, neighing. The other bolted before the second got his feet back on the ground, and the reins snapped. The second one stumbled, and with another wave of panic, they both bolted again, ripping the reins out of Jasper's hands.

Pain washed through Jasper's arm and shoulder, shooting through his muscles. His arm went dead, sticking out funny, and he couldn't move it. He knew immediately that he'd dislocated it. He'd seen it happen to another farmer years ago. He knew what it looked like.

What he hadn't known was how it felt.

Now he did.

And he never wanted to feel that kind of pain ever again.

He cried out, clutching his arm close.

The horses lunged forward several more times as the men continued moving the stones around. Then, with a final burst of strength, everyone managed to free the wagon from the muddy bottom of the river. It rolled forward on the rocks and through the debris in the water. The horses soon trudged on ahead through the water.

With his dislocated shoulder screaming in pain, he struggled to the shore, the current was tugging on his legs, and by the time he reached the sand, he collapsed. The pain overtook him. Dr. Evans rushed toward him, dropping to his knees as he reached Jasper. A few other men surrounded them while the rest stayed with the German couple, ensuring they were all right on the other side of the river.

"It's dislocated," Jasper said to him through grit teeth. He hissed with his words. "I know it is."

Dr. Evans examined his injured shoulder, breathing out a deep breath. "Well, you aren't wrong, unfortunately. It is dislocated, and I've got to put it back into place."

"How painful will that be?"

"How much pain are you in now?"

"I'm about to pass out."

"Well, I hate to say it, but you still might as I'm setting it."

Jasper looked up at the doctor. Dread warmed through his chest. He hated pain, but worse than that, he hated when others saw him in pain. "Can you do me a favor?"

"Anything."

"Don't let Miss Randall see me pass out."

Dr. Evans chuckled and then looked toward the rest of the wagon train. The men had returned from checking on the German couple, while the women—including Miss Callahan and the rest of the women traveling with her—all had begun to climb down from their wagons and make their way toward the commotion. Although no one was close to the two men just yet, they would be soon, and Dr. Evans held up his hand, stopping anyone from coming to the aid. "It's all right. Just stay where you are." He looked down at Jasper, dropping his voice to a whisper. "I'll keep her away."

"Thanks."

"All right. Are you ready?" Dr. Evans grabbed Jasper's elbow and shoulder.

"I suppose so."

"As hard as it will be, you need to relax as much as possible and let me do the work."

Jasper gritted his teeth and nodded as he braced himself. With a firm grip on Jasper's arm, Dr. Evans applied a sudden and forceful pressure to the dislocated joint, twisting it. Jasper screamed out, the pain almost too much to bear. Suddenly, with a loud pop, the joint slid back into place.

The world began to spin, and Jasper closed his eyes, fighting for consciousness. He wanted to lie down, but he knew he couldn't.

"It's in. It's over. Are you awake?"

"Barely."

"Well, at least you didn't pass out."

Dr. Evans opened his doctor bag, yanking out a tourniquet, and began wrapping Jasper's arm and shoulder. After stabilizing it, he tied the end and tucked it under to secure the knot. Jasper lay there, and he closed his eyes as he tried to catch his breath and steady his racing heart.

Once Dr. Evans was satisfied that the shoulder was properly stabilized, he sat back and wiped the sweat from his forehead. "All right, Jasper, you'll be sore for a while, but the shoulder should heal up just fine. You'll need to take it easy for a few days and avoid any heavy lifting or strenuous activity."

Jasper snorted. "You mean strenuous activity like traveling across the country in a wagon?"

"Kind of." Dr. Evans laid his hand on Jasper's good shoulder. "I'll help you get your wagon across the river as soon as I get my wife across."

"Sounds good." Jasper nodded, relieved that the worst was over and the world had stopped spinning around him. He sat up. "Thank you for the help, Dr. Evans," he said, his voice rough with pain.

Dr. Evans smiled. "Don't thank me until we get your supplies across the river and your camp set up. That's going to be the hardest part of today."

~

CORA

Cora bit her lip as Winona stirred the stew cooking on the fire. Although the rest of the wagons had made it across the river without any other difficulties, the stress of the whole day seemed to take hold of her senses, and she stared off into the growing darkness that surrounded the camp. With far too many thoughts in her head, her mind jumped from one to another to another, never allowing her a moment's peace. She flinched at every sound, and as Winona stood and faced her, she closed her eyes for a second, inhaling a sharp breath.

"Are you all right?" the headmistress asked her.

"Yeah. Fine. I just don't like the dark anymore."

"I understand."

Although Cora wanted to snort, she didn't. Doing so would be rude. The problem was that she doubted the headmistress really understood. Sure, she had her own fears for all the young women on the wagon train, but she didn't have Cora's fear. She hadn't felt a man's fingers tight around her throat as he tried to squeeze the life out of her.

"Are you hungry?" Winona asked.

"Not really."

"You should still try to eat."

"I know."

Winona cocked her head to the side and reached out, clutching Cora's elbow. "Why don't you take some to Mr. Scott? Lark mentioned that Carter had helped Mr. Scott set up camp after he got the wagon across the river, and she seemed to think that although he was all right, he was too sore to do much for himself. I think he would appreciate the help."

Cora bit her lip again. She hadn't spoken to Jasper since the night he saved her from Sam. Of course, she had wanted to. But every time she tried, something always stopped her. She didn't know why. Perhaps it was because she feared that he blamed her for what happened, or worse, hated her for it.

What if he never wanted to see or speak to her again?

"I suppose I could."

"Good. I'll get you a bowl and fill it for you."

Before Cora could think about what she had agreed to, Winona grabbed a bowl, filled it almost to the brim with stew, and handed it to her. "Tell him if he wants more; he just needs to ask. In fact, tell him if he would like to just come over to my wagon for all his meals, then he's more than welcome."

Cora glanced at the ground, and her stomach twisted.

"What's the matter? Don't you want me to invite him?" Winona lifted one eyebrow.

"It's not that. I . . . I haven't spoken to him about everything that happened. I don't know what he's thinking."

"Well, I'm sure you'll know after you take him the stew."

"I guess so."

Before Cora could blink, Winona was shooing her away from the wagon and telling her not to forget to let Mr. Scott know he was welcome to join them.

Cora inhaled a deep breath, holding it for a few strides as she made her way over to his wagon. She found him sitting by the fire, staring at the flames as they licked at a chunk of wood in the middle of them. It hadn't been in the fire long enough, and most of the bark was still a light brown.

"Jasper?" Cora asked as she approached, a slight bit of hesitation hinted in her voice.

He blinked and looked up at her. "Cora?" He stood, wincing. "How are you?"

"I'm all right. How are you?" She motioned toward his arm.

He shrugged. "I'm fine."

"Does it hurt?"

"Not anymore. It's just sore. Dr. Evans said that will go away in a few days." Jasper pointed toward the blanket lying on the ground near the fire. "Would you care to sit for a moment?"

"Sure."

Once they were both seated, she handed him the bowl. "Here. Winona wanted you to have this."

"Oh. Thank you." He took the bowl, pointing toward another one by the fire. "The German woman brought me over something a few minutes ago. I have to admit that while it does smell all right, I don't know what's in it. To be honest, it kind of scares me."

Cora leaned forward, sniffing at the bowl, while she moved the spoon around and lifted a spoonful to examine it. Jasper was right; it smelled all right. But there was a difference to it that gave it an odd look.

"It was a nice thought," Jasper said. "But I can't lie and say I hadn't decided just to go hungry tonight."

"I don't blame you. I'm not sure I could eat it either."

They both laughed, and the tension in Cora's shoulders softened. Or, at least, it did until she thought about it. She trained her gaze on the fire as she fiddled with her fingers.

Jasper watched her for a moment then the smile vanished from his face. He cleared his throat. "I've been meaning to see how you've been. I'm sorry I haven't been able to talk to you much."

"It's all right. You were with Mr. Mills, looking for . . ." Unable to say Sam's name, she let her voice trail off, and she paused slightly before continuing. "Then we were traveling."

"I had planned to ask you how you've been at the funeral, but I didn't see you."

"I stayed in the wagon. I couldn't go."

"I understand."

Silence fell over them until Cora glanced at the bowl of stew still in Jasper's hand. "You should eat that before it gets cold."

He nodded and reached for the spoon inside the German woman's bowl. After wiping it off, he dug into Winona's hot meal, shoveling bites into his mouth with one hand while he struggled to hold the bowl with the other.

"Here, let me hold it for you," she whispered, taking it from him.

He looked into her eyes, and her heart thumped.

"About what happened . . ." He paused, finishing a bite. "I'm sorry you had to go through what you did."

"It wasn't your fault."

"I know. But I'm still sorry."

"I shouldn't have trusted him. It was foolish of me."

"You shouldn't look at it that way. You were not the fool. He was."

Although she wanted to believe Jasper, there was a big part of her that couldn't. She'd been so caught up in the quest for love and marriage that she'd ignored her gut feeling when it came to the likes of Sam Wright. She'd been nothing but a stupid girl, making stupid choices.

"If he was, I was. There were things I noticed that I wasn't sure of, and Winona didn't like him, at least not fully. She did . . . er does like you, though." As the words left Cora's lip, her cheeks flushed with heat. She had said what she did without thinking about it first.

"Oh really?" Jasper chuckled. "I suppose I should be honored then." He cocked his head to the side, closing one eye as he leaned back. "Although, I'm not sure I feel comfortable with you talking about me. What did y'all say?"

"We weren't talking about you."

"You just said she liked me, so obviously something was said."

"She just asked about you, and I told her how we met."

"There sounds like there is an 'and' missing from your sentence." He chuckled.

"There is no and . . . well, I suppose when she asked about your plans, I mentioned California and how you wanted to pan for gold. When she asked about your plans for marriage, I told her you weren't thinking about it."

"That's not true."

"It's not?"

"Well, I suppose it was. But now . . ."

"Now what?"

"Well, I suppose that depends on how you feel?"

His eyes bore into hers, and she got lost in their intensity. Then, without thinking, she leaned in and pressed her lips to his. He responded eagerly, wrapping his hand around her neck and pulling her close. Her heart raced as she deepened the kiss, her fingers tangling in his hair until the sudden realization of what she was doing smacked her.

She shouldn't be kissing him! What on earth was she thinking?

She pulled away and covered her lips with her fingers.

"What's the matter?" he asked.

She shook her head and rose to her feet. "I should get back to the wagon."

"Wait!" Jasper stood, nearly losing his balance in his haste. "Was it something I did?"

"No." She shook her head, feeling her cheeks flush again. "I just . . . I should get back to my wagon." With a slight giggle, she trotted off, not knowing if she should be happy or embarrassed. She didn't know what to make of anything; however, she did know that one thing was for certain—nothing would ever be quite the same again for either of them.

Not after tonight.

FIFTEEN

JASPER

Fort Laramie was once a fur trade post that had now turned into a military garrison, and as Jasper's gaze traced over the fort's high walls, he couldn't help but feel a sense of relief. The wagon train had spent several long days on the trail, pushing their horses and wagons—and sometimes their sanity—to a breaking point to get here, and while he didn't know how long Mr. Mills planned to camp, he hoped they would stay at least a few days, resting and resupplying for the long stretch to Fort Hall.

Fort Hall, Jasper thought. What will I do then?

He hadn't thought of his plans since the night Cora had brought him supper. It wasn't that he hadn't wanted to; it was that he couldn't without wanting to squirm right out of his own body. But, when he left Missouri, he had had a plan. He was going to leave the wagon train at Fort Hall and head to California. Period. End of the story. Well, in a manner of speaking. Surely, he hoped that the move to the state would bring him a new life, a new beginning, and a new story, but figuratively speaking, that was the end of the line, the end goal, the end of the story.

But now that story had a kink.

Like a broken chain or ripped seam on a wagon hitch line that unraveled so much the rein was useless.

Of course, many men in the world would tell him that a woman couldn't or shouldn't be compared to a broken chain. A woman, and the love of one, was something to be cherished, leaving a man with the feeling of an utter blessing from God.

It wasn't that he was saying Cora wasn't those things, but after he'd had his heart set on something for so long, the sudden idea of those plans changing had just sent his mind into a tailspin.

He'd always thought love was for the weak, the kind of thing poets and fools wrote about. But ever since he had met Cora, everything had changed. He had started to feel things he never thought were possible like his heart beating faster every time he heard her voice or the way his palms got sweaty when she was near him. He had tried to push those feelings aside, thinking that his goal of getting to California was more important than any fleeting emotions, but as the days went on, he couldn't ignore them any longer.

He couldn't deny the attraction he felt towards her, and now that they had shared a kiss . . .

He just would never be the same.

Not after that.

He had noticed her on the wagon train from the first night after they left Independence, but he had kept his distance. He didn't want any distractions on his way to California. But as the days went by, he found himself drawn to her. Her smile, her laugh, how she looked at him—it was all starting to become too much to resist.

And he didn't want to do it any longer.

He didn't know what would happen to his plans to go to California, but he did know that no matter where they ended up, he wanted them to be together.

Now, all he had to do was hope and pray she felt the same.

As the wagon train drew closer to the fort, Jasper could see the bustling activity of soldiers and traders going about their business. The sound of horses neighing and men shouting filled the air, and he almost couldn't wait to rest his weary bones and take a break from the monotonous routine of traveling day in and day out. He almost couldn't wait to dismount and stretch his legs.

Mr. Mills veered everyone off to the side, and after they circled the wagons and Jasper set up his camp, he grabbed his bag with his good arm and set off for the fort, glancing over his shoulder several times in the hope that no one saw him. Part of him wished to wait and see if Cora wanted to go, yet there was also something he wanted to do, and he needed to be alone to do it.

~

Much like Fort Kearney, Fort Laramie was a bustle of people. Men, women, and children all meandered throughout the fort, taking in the business dealings of buying fresh supplies or enjoying a hot meal at one of the many meal tents. A few children with the adults ran around the tables between bites of food while the parents looked on.

While most of the families stayed toward the front of the fort, there were a few men who seemed to stay toward the back near the liquor tents, and as Jasper passed one, he could smell the whiskey as it permeated every inch of canvas and every inch of any man who dared go into the place. He could hear the roars of laughter of the men inside even as he continued toward several more tents along the outskirts of the fort.

With every face he passed, Jasper searched for Mr. Wright. He wasn't sure what he would do if he saw the man. Especially considering he only had one working arm while the other one was still wrapped to his side, but at this point, nothing was stopping Jasper from doing whatever he thought he should at the moment. Not to mention, there were enough military soldiers around; surely, justice would be awaiting the murderer either way.

Jasper continued toward several tents located near the middle of the fort. While these offered supplies, it wasn't the usual beans and flour type of goods. These tents were for trinkets and other home goods that travelers often sold for money when they needed it, and as Jasper entered the first tent, he looked around at all the shelves full of hand-held mirrors, jewelry boxes, trunks, clothes, boots, pots, pans, dishes, and even guns and knives—all items that had meant something to someone until they needed money for food more.

Jasper searched around, looking for something in particular, but not seeing it anywhere.

Surely, there would be some for sale, right, he wondered. It wasn't like no one would be willing to sell theirs for the right price—especially if they needed money for food.

He made his way around the tent, and upon not finding what he was looking for, he meandered up to the makeshift counter. The man standing behind it eyed him for a moment.

"You look like you can't find what you're looking for," the man said. A slight smirk spread across his face.

"No, sir, I can't."

The man scratched his dirt-stained chin as he raised one eyebrow. A slight hesitation purred through his tone. "Well, what is it that you are looking for? Maybe I've got it, but it's just not out."

"I'm looking for a ring." Jasper's heart thumped as he spoke.

"Like a wedding ring?"

"Yeah."

The man glanced around at the few other people in the tent,

eyeing them for a second before he bent down and yanked a wooden box from under the table he probably considered a counter. He opened the box, exposing several gold bands lying on a bed of black velvet. "None of them got any diamonds, but they are pure. I've checked them myself."

"Nice. Thank you."

Jasper leaned over, looking through all of the bands. Some were large, and he imagined they would fit a man, while the rest were small. Dainty is the word that came to mind, and as he looked through them, the sudden realization that he didn't know what size to buy hit him like a train barreling down the tracks.

His heart thumped harder.

"Do you like one in particular?" the man asked. He looked at Jasper as though he sensed Jasper's sudden hesitation.

"Oh, yes, I do. I like this one, but it's just . . . well, I don't know what size she would wear."

He heard a woman giggle behind him, and he froze.

Lord, please, let it not be her, he thought.

His blood ran cold, and although he didn't want to, he glanced over his shoulder, bracing himself for the chance of seeing Cora standing in the tent, watching him as he looked at a wedding ring for her.

Miss McCall and Miss Linwell met his gaze as they stood behind him. They both covered their mouths with their hands.

His breathing quickened, and his gaze darted around the tent.

"She's not with us," Miss McCall said.

"Fortunately for you," Miss Linwell added.

The two women giggled again, and although relief washed through him, his senses were still on edge. While Cora still didn't know what he was doing, they did.

Miss McCall stepped forward, making her way toward him

as she cocked her head to the side. She looked down at the rings as she laid her hand on his shoulder. "I think Cora would like that one," she said, pointing to a band with a slightly beveled edge engraved around the whole thing. It was the one he had picked.

Heat rushed up the back of his neck, and a lump formed in his throat. He tried to swallow it but couldn't, and it made his voice crack as he spoke. "I thought so too. But I don't know if it would fit her."

"Well, let's see. I think she and I have about the same size hands." Miss Linwell looked at the man behind the counter. "May I?"

"Of course."

As soon as he gave his permission, she picked up the ring and slid it on her left ring finger. "It's perfect. I think it would fit her."

"And what if it doesn't?" Jasper asked.

"Then you will find another one when you reach Oregon. But she could have this one for now."

"I suppose that's a good plan."

Miss Linwell slipped the ring off and handed it to him as she winked. "And don't worry. We won't tell her."

The two women giggled a third time, and after they walked away, moving toward the other side of the tent where they went through a couple of stacks of dresses, Jasper turned back to the man, asking. "How much?"

"Fifty dollars."

Jasper set the ring on the counter and dug into his pants, yanking out the last of his money. While the ring certainly didn't take it all, it dented what he had left. Now there wasn't any question about him having to find gold to keep his supplies up. Of course, Cora was worth it. He'd just have to get a little better about finding enough to make a life for them.

He didn't want her to go without anything from this day forward.

With the ring tucked in his pocket, Jasper accompanied Miss Linwell and Miss McCall around to the other supply tents, helping them buy what they needed and buying what he knew he needed. By the time they were finished, a thin layer of sweat had glistened on his forehead and the back of his neck, and he yanked his handkerchief from his pocket and wiped it all away.

"So, when do you think you'll ask her?" Miss McCall asked as they made their way toward the fort gates, headed back to camp.

He shrugged. "I don't know." He paused, squinting as he looked up toward the sky. "I'm not sure how she even feels about marrying me."

"I'm certain she will say yes." Miss McCall brushed her hand against her shoulder. "I wouldn't worry if I were you."

"Thank you for the confidence, Miss McCall."

"You may call me Harper. If you want, that is. And this is Grace." She snorted a slight chuckle as she pointed to Miss Linwell. "I mean, it only makes sense since Cora is like a sister, and you two are going to marry . . . well, I suppose that would make you a brother-in-law."

"I suppose it does too."

The three of them continued toward the gate, and as they rounded the corner, Jasper nearly ran into Mr. Mills, who stood, talking to a man that towered over everyone.

Both women sucked in their breath, skidding to a stop along with Jasper.

"Sorry, Mr. Mills," Jasper said.

"It's not a problem, Mr. Scott." The wagon master pointed to the man standing with him. "In fact, I'm glad I ran into you. This is Mr. Campbell, and he's a blacksmith. He's agreed to join us to Oregon, so we don't have to worry about horses throwing shoes or breaking any bits. He also knows how to fix the steel rings on the wagon wheels."

Jasper looked at Mr. Campbell, who stuck out his hand. "Nice to meet you," Mr. Campbell said. "The name is Brooks Campbell."

"Jasper Scott." The two men shook hands. "So, you're a blacksmith. That will come in handy on the trail."

"Well, at least I know my work will be important." Mr. Campbell chuckled and then glanced at the two women with Jasper. "Ladies." He tipped his hat.

Harper was the first to step forward, and she held out her hand for him to shake. "Mr. Campbell," she said. A broad grin inched across her face, and her cheeks flushed a slight shade of pink. Grace shook his hand too but didn't say much other than it was nice to meet the blacksmith before she retreated a few steps behind Harper and Jasper, dropping her gaze as she tucked her blonde hair behind her ears.

Mr. Mills glanced between them and rested his hands on his hips. "Well, Mr. Campbell, we should let you get back to your wagon. You may join us anytime. I wanted to give everyone a few days' rest before we head out. Does that work for you?"

"Sure." Mr. Campbell nodded. "Just let me know when and I'll be ready."

As the three bid farewell to the wagon master and the blacksmith, they turned back toward the camp. Mrs. Evans and Cora were running for them, waving their arms, and as the two women reached them, they both bent over to catch their breath.

"Harper. Grace. We need you two to come back to camp." Mrs. Evans said, pointing toward the wagons in the distance.

"What is it?" Harper asked.

"It's the German woman, Mrs. Schneider. She's in labor. Carter needs our help."

Jasper's heart leaped as Cora looked from the two women to him, and he could feel the ring burn a hole in his pocket. She smiled at him, waving slightly before she darted off with the rest of the ladies back to camp.

Tonight, Jasper thought. *I'll ask her to marry me tonight.*

SIXTEEN

CORA

Seeing Jasper had caused a flutter in Cora's stomach, and she wanted nothing more than to speak to him. Unfortunately, she knew Mrs. Schneider needed her more, or at least Lark and Carter needed her. Given that she'd never helped a woman give birth before, she doubted she could do anything for Mrs. Schneider that Carter couldn't.

Part of her had even wondered why Lark had asked them to help.

Cora followed the other three women back to the German couple's wagon, arriving just as Carter was coming from the back. His shirt sleeves were rolled up, and he carried two buckets, one in each hand.

"Can one of you fill these?" he asked them.

Cora raised her hand, moving forward first. "I'll do it."

"I'll help her," Harper said, reaching for one of the buckets while Cora grabbed the other.

"Try to hurry." Carter motioned toward the river, then turned to Lark and Grace. "I need one of you to find a stick for her to bite down on and the other one to go to the fort and try to find Mr. Schneider. He went to buy supplies this morning and hasn't returned."

"I'll go find him," Grace said. "I was just inside the fort. I know where all the supply tents are."

She darted off just as Cora and Harper trotted away from the camp toward the river. Lark stayed behind with her husband.

"So, how was the fort?" Cora asked as she hurried after Harper. The bucket in her hand swung back and forth, banging into her hip every few strides.

"It was fine." Harper glanced over her shoulder. "There were a lot of people there."

"Why were you with Jasper?"

"We saw him at one of the tents, and he helped us."

The two young women arrived at the river and scurried down to the water's edge. Harper looked at Cora, smiling as though she knew the thoughts swirling around Cora's mind. "Don't worry. He only has eyes for you." A slight chuckle whispered through Harper's words.

"And what is that supposed to mean? Cora laid her hand on her hip as a hint of amusement beat in her chest.

"He likes you."

"Did he say anything?"

Harper shook her head. "He didn't have to. I could tell."

Cora bit her lip. She didn't know if she could confess about the kiss or not. Surely, Harper wouldn't judge Cora for her actions. Nor would she tell her she needed to tell Winona or lecture her on how inappropriate it was. But she also knew that the more people who knew, the greater risk that Winona would find out.

"Don't you like him too?" Harper asked, raising one eyebrow.

"Yes, I do."

"So, what's with the face?" Harper pointed her finger toward Cora and swirled it as though drawing a circle in the air.

"It's just . . . I kissed him last night." Cora closed her eyes, bracing for Harper's surprise. When the young woman didn't say anything nor make a sound, Cora opened her eyes and saw Harper standing in front of her, staring with her mouth gaped."

"You kissed him?"

"Yes."

"And what happened?"

"Well, I panicked and left."

Harper laughed, and Cora slapped the young woman on the shoulder. "It's not funny."

"Oh, but it is."

"I should have talked to him, but we were in a hurry."

"It's all right. You can talk to him later."

"If he will even talk to me. I can't imagine what he's thinking after I left so quickly."

Harper laughed again, brushing her hand over Cora's shoulder and down her arm. "Trust me; he isn't thinking anything other than how much he likes you."

The two women said nothing more as they filled the buckets and returned to the wagon. Although Cora wanted to believe Harper, a little voice in the back of her head kept nagging at her, telling her not to be so trusting of another's words. She always hated when doubt played tricks on her, and this time was no different.

If I could just talk to him, she thought. *Then I could see what he was thinking.*

But could she be the first one to say something?

Doubtful.

Perhaps it would be best for him to broach the subject first. That way, there would be less chance of making things awkward between them. It was already bad enough that she kissed him; she didn't want to send a prescient that she was always the one who made the first move.

Why did I kiss him? She wanted to smack her own forehead, but she also didn't want to make a scene in front of anyone. The less Harper knew that she thought about the whole thing, the less likely the young woman would bring it up again or, worse, talk about it with Grace or Lark. The last thing Cora needed was those two knowing too.

The two made their way back to the wagon, and by the time they reached it, Grace had found Mr. Schneider. The man was pacing outside the wagon while his wife moaned and cried. He mumbled words in German, throwing his hands up in the air every few steps. Mr. Mills and Winona had come by to check on the situation, and although they were trying to calm Mr. Schneider, their efforts were proving more fruitless than not.

"He's just worried about his wife," Winona said to the women as they watched the man with wide eyes.

"How is Mrs. Schneider doing?" Harper asked.

"She's doing fine. Carter is helping as best as he can, but her English is . . ." Winona shrugged. "She only knows a few words, and most aren't any that he needs to use in this situation. Supper, breakfast, supplies, money—not exactly the phrases a doctor would use when delivering a baby." A slight chuckle whispered through Winona's chest.

"Perhaps I can help." Harper moved forward, and Winona grabbed her arm.

"How do you think you're going to do that? You can't speak German."

"Yes, I know. But I have taught children how to read and speak."

"Just let her try, Winona," Grace said, folding her arms across her chest.

Winona nodded, and Harper made her way around to the back of the wagon. "Can I help?" she asked.

Although Cora couldn't hear what Carter said, as Harper vanished behind the bonnet, Cora assumed he had agreed.

∼

"*Es ist ein junge!*" Mr. Schneider ran out from behind the wagon with his newborn infant in his arms. He held up the tiny, wrapped body, and the rest of the wagon train clapped. A broad grin spread across his face. "*Es ist ein junge!*"

"What does that mean?" Winona asked Cora and Harper.

They shrugged, and the headmistress moved toward the man after not getting the answer she wanted.

"Is it a boy or a girl?" she asked him.

"*Es ist ein junge.*"

She nodded. "I heard you. But I don't know . . ." She motioned toward the infant. "May I see it?"

Mr. Schnieder looked at her. "*Ich verstehe nicht.*"

She pointed toward herself. "I . . . me. May I . . ." She pointed to her eye and then the baby. "See the baby?" She repeated the move and question twice until Mr. Schneider finally understood and nodded.

"*Ja. Ja.*"

He lowered the infant and then handed it to her, and as she cradled it in her arms, she opened the blanket. "It's a boy," she told everyone gathered around. She looked at him. "Boy."

"*Ja. Junge.*" He smiled again and then tried to say the word. "B . . . B . . . Boooy."

"Yes. Boy. And he's adorable."

Mr. Schneider cocked his head to the side. "Ador . . ador . ."

Winona bit her lip. "Um. He's . . . perfect. Do you know perfect?"

"I think . . . so. Perfect. Yes. Perfect."

The rest of the wagon train moved closer, and while the men

kept their distance from the baby, instead opting to shake the new father's hand and wish him a heartfelt congratulations, the women surrounded Winona. Cora heard more *oohs* and *aahs* than she'd ever heard, but as she looked down upon the tiny infant, even her heart gushed slightly.

"He's so little," she said to the headmistress.

"Yes, he is. It's hard to believe we all start this little." She smiled. "Do you want to hold him?"

Cora nodded, taking the baby into her arms. He squirmed, and his face scrunched briefly before settling and falling back asleep. He had a full head of black hair that stuck out in all directions, and he sucked on his lip. Cora's heart swelled. She'd never seen anything so perfect, and it was as if time stood still. She thought of how it would feel if the baby was hers, and it was all she could do to keep herself from tearing up.

She knew she had longed for love and marriage, but she hadn't thought about children. It was the one thing she never thought of and the one thing she now wanted more than anything.

She yearned to be a wife.

But she yearned more to be a mother.

She looked up at Winona and saw Jasper, who stood not far from them, looking at her as she held the baby. He smiled and nodded, and the look on his face sent another rush of longing to flutter in her chest. The memory of his lips on hers was already burned into her mind, and looking at him looking at her now only made it more powerful.

Grace and Harper moved up alongside her, taking in the precious sight while Lark hung back, watching the women from a distance.

"Lark?" Winona asked. "Do you want to hold the baby?"

Lark shook her head. "That's not necessary."

"Oh, sure it is." Winona took the baby from Cora and handed

him to Lark, who took the infant in a stiff and awkward way. "There. See. You look quite lovely with a baby in your arms."

Carter jumped down from the wagon and made his way over to the crowd as he wiped his hands with a rag. Upon seeing his wife with the baby, he smiled.

"That's a good look," he said to her.

"Yeah, well, don't get used to it just yet." She turned a bright shade of pink and then turned, handing the baby back to Winona. "You can have him back."

Winona took the child, giving him one last tap on his nose with her finger before handing him back to his father, who took him, nodded a thank you to everyone, then took the child back to his mother. The crowd around Winona and the baby dwindled, leaving the women and the doctor standing near the German couple's wagon. Lark's eyes were unfocused, giving her a far-off look that Cora had seen before when something was troubling her. Cora wanted to relish in it, but when she tried, she couldn't. No matter what they'd already been through or how she'd felt about the woman in the past, at that moment, she had this overwhelming urge to hug the woman she once thought of as an enemy. The problem was, she didn't know why.

"Are you all right?" Carter asked his wife.

She dropped her gaze to the ground and nodded. "I just forgot. I needed to get started on supper."

Before she could say another word, she spun and walked off. Carter looked at Winona and shrugged. "She's been . . . reluctant to talk about children," he said to the headmistress.

"I don't doubt that she would be given her upbringing."

"I just . . . want her to know that she doesn't have anything to fear. But I can't reason with her."

"Give it time, Carter. She is just finding her ground."

"I just hope that no matter where she finds it, she finds it with me."

"She will."

Carter ran his hands through his hair. "I should get back to Mrs. Schneider. I want to check on her one more time before I leave them be for the night." The women watched him vanish around the other side of the wagon, and Winona exhaled a deep breath.

WINONA

Unsure of what was going on with Lark, Winona made her way to the wagon Lark shared with her husband with caution. Her mind reeled with all the possibilities, and while she wanted to ignore any gut feelings, there was one that plagued her the most—so much that it nagged her to the point where she couldn't not think about it.

Was there trouble in their marriage, or was Lark regretting getting married?

She didn't want to think it, much less entertain the notion that's what could be wrong with the woman, but it also ate at her to no end.

Approaching the wagon, a lump caught in her throat, and although she tried to swallow it, she couldn't. It lodged itself too tight and wouldn't budge. She hadn't fully known why she had asked for the job at hand, but she hoped that Lark wouldn't tell her to leave before she had a chance to at least try to help.

"Lark?" she called out, stopping near the campfire.

Lark moved around the wagon, and she halted in her tracks. The buckets in her arms swung from her sudden change of movement. "What are you doing here?" she asked.

"I came to see if you were all right."

Lark chewed on her lip. "I'm fine."

"Really? Because you seemed upset while you were holding the baby. Is something going on?" Winona didn't want to tell her about what Carter said in case it would make Lark mad. Sure, she hated holding that information from the woman, but she thought it best that she did. "Is it something with Carter? Did something happen between the two of you?"

"No." She shook her head, staring at the headmistress until finally, she dropped the buckets, letting her shoulders hunch. "It's just that he's just been asking about children and I . . . I don't know what to say."

"Well, it's not really up to you." Winona snorted.

"I know it's not. Or at least in a manner of speaking. I learned long ago what a woman should do if she doesn't want a child at the bordello."

Winona's heart sank, and she pressed her fingertips against her lips. She didn't even want to think about what Lark was suggesting. "But you wouldn't do that, would you?" A hint of panic etched in her voice, and it cracked.

"No, I wouldn't. At least, I don't think I would."

"Good, because I don't think you should."

"But what if I'm a terrible mother?"

"I don't think that is possible. Look at all the children you helped care for at the orphanage."

"Yes, but they weren't mine. They weren't my responsibility."

"So? You still took care of them, and you loved them, which is all they needed, and it's all your children will need too."

Lark looked up at the sky. Her eyes misted with tears, and she sniffed as though she could start crying any moment. She bit her lip and glanced back at Winona. "I guess no matter what I think, though, I'll find out . . . soon."

Winona slapped her hand across her mouth as she stared at Lark. Before Lark could say anything else, Winona rushed toward her, wrapping her arms around Lark's neck. "Are you sure?"

"I think so."

"Does Carter know?"

"No. But he will soon as the weeks continue and I'm late in my courses."

Winona's heart fluttered.

A baby.

The first in their little makeshift family.

It was just one more dream come true, and she could burst; she was so full of excitement. "When do you think you will tell him?"

Lark shrugged. "I'm not sure. I thought I should wait until I know for certain if I am or if I'm not. I know he'll be thrilled. I'm just not sure if I can share in those feelings just yet."

"Well, no matter what happens, I want you to know that I love you, and I think you will be an amazing mother," she whispered.

SEVENTEEN

WINONA

Winona sat by the campfire, watching all the wagon train travelers celebrate the Schneider family's happy addition. While most danced and sang to the music a few of the men played, the rest sat around the huge campfire, swapping stories and enjoying a meal of steak, potatoes, and cornbread. Although she sat alone, watching everyone around her have the time of their lives, she didn't care. She was on cloud nine, and there wasn't anything short of someone dying—even if that was a morbid thought—that could wipe the smile from her face.

Not after hearing the news that Lark could be with child.

It was just too perfect of news.

"You seem like you're in a rather good mood," a voice said behind her.

She looked up as Mr. Mills stepped over the log she was sitting on and sat beside her.

"I am in one," she said. "And there's nothing you can do that will change that."

"Nothing I can do?" He leaned away from her, widening his eyes. "You make it sound like I make you miserable.

"Well, you can't deny that our last conversation didn't go well. In fact, I'm not sure I remember one that has."

"I don't know what you're talking about. I've been a perfect gentleman every time we've spoken." He cocked his head to the side and winked.

"A perfect gentleman, huh? I think I would beg to differ."

"Yeah, you're probably right." He stretched his arms above his head simultaneously as he stretched his legs out in front of him. He groaned loudly, pulling his limbs back into his body before moving off the log and crouching near the fire. He grabbed a nearby stick, poking at the chunk of burning wood with a stick. Flecks of ash floated around the campfire and landed in the grass, turning black and smoking as they extinguished.

Winona brushed her wisps of hair away from her face. "It was quite an eventful day for the camp and for Mr. and Mrs. Schneider. I'm surprised you missed it."

He cleared his throat and tossed the stick aside before standing. He wiped his hands together, brushed off whatever was on them, and adjusted his pants around his waist. "I can guarantee you, Miss Callahan, that neither of them needed my help or needed me around. I wouldn't know the first thing about babies or bringing them into the world." He glanced down at the ground, nodding as his shoulders softened.

"Really?" She cocked her head to the side, raising one eyebrow. "I would think there would be lots of babies born on these wagon trains."

"I suppose there have been a few over the years, but I've never paid much attention to them. It's not really my business."

"Don't you hold them at least?"

"Nope. Never have held a single one."

She tucked her hair behind her ears. "I don't think I could stand not holding them. Truth be told, it was rather nice to hold an infant again today. I didn't know how much I had missed the orphanage until now."

"Did you never wish to marry or have children of your own?"

Winona didn't know what shocked her more, his question or that he was even asking it in the first place.

"I did. But it just wasn't in the cards for me. I suppose God had other plans, and I was needed someplace else more."

"I can understand that. I was never one for marriage or love myself. I always had too much to think about. Perhaps I'll regret it one day, but I can't say that day is today." He chuckled.

"I suppose in the end, I did get a family in the four young women traveling with me. They are, without a doubt, like my own daughters. I can't wait to see them all married with children of their own. Perhaps then I can finally know the joy of being a grandmother." She inhaled another breath, blowing it out through her nose as she remembered her conversation with Lark.

Lord, I pray there is a baby on the way, she thought.

So many of her dreams were wrapped up in this one moment, this one trip. Heading to Oregon could either be everything they'd ever hoped for or their worst nightmare, and she prayed it wouldn't be the latter. "Of course, that is if we get to Oregon safely."

Mr. Mills furrowed his brow briefly, looking down and then back at her. "I don't make many promises in life, Miss Callahan, but I will promise that I'll do everything I can to get you and those women safely to Oregon. You have my word."

"Good. I'm going to hold you to that," she said.

CORA

Cora meandered through the crowd celebrating around the campfire. Everyone seemed in a joyous mood, whether it was because of the new addition to the Schneider family or perhaps they were simply excited for a few days' rest from the trail. Either way, it didn't matter. She could see both reasons for celebration.

While Harper and Grace were singing with the Reed family, Lark and Carter had found their seats with Mr. Mills and Winona. The four of them seemed lost in a conversation that Cora couldn't hear and, frankly, didn't mind not hearing. She wasn't in the mood for talk of what had been happening to the wagon train or even about the Oregon trail itself.

In fact, when this adventure was finally done, if she never saw a wagon again in her life, she'd be grateful—even if the trail had brought some good things for her.

"Cora?" a voice said behind her. She spun to find Jasper waving as he leaned against a nearby wagon. With his one arm still wrapped to his side, he waved at her with his other hand.

Her heart fluttered, and as she made her way over to him, warmth spread up the back of her neck. She hadn't exactly planned what she would say to him, and she hoped she wouldn't stumble over her words.

"Great party, huh?" he asked, pointing toward a few of the husbands and wives now dancing in a circle along with the music. Their children clapped as they watched.

"It is."

"Have you eaten yet?" He motioned toward the big pot of stew hanging on the campfire.

"I haven't, but I'm not hungry right now."

"Yeah, I'm not either." He shoved his hand in his pocket and hunched his shoulders slightly as though he meant to shorten his frame. A thinned smile inched across his face, and his gaze danced around. "I saw you after the baby was born, holding it . . . him."

"He is cute, isn't he?"

"He is. Well, from what I could tell. I was standing a little too far away to really see him."

"I haven't held a baby in a long time. We had a few over the years at the orphanage. Us, older women, always tried to help Winona when we could."

"I bet living there was like having a bunch of siblings." He snorted a laugh.

There was something off about him. Like he was overly nervous or something, and Cora couldn't put her finger on what it was. She feared that it was because of the kiss. Had he wished she hadn't kissed him?

"It was. Although, at times, I wondered if such was a good thing or not. I'm not sure if you ever fought with your brothers, but siblings can share in a disagreement every now and then."

"My brothers and I fought every day. I understand exactly what you mean."

Silence fell between them, and they both watched the crowd. While Cora didn't know if he did because he was uncomfortable with their conversation, she fought with herself on whether or not to say anything.

"Cora, do you think we could go somewhere alone to talk?" He hooked his thumb over his shoulder, and the sudden change in his tone sent her pulse racing.

"Sure."

She followed behind him, trying to ignore how she could hear her heartbeat in her ears. Her breathing quickened, and she feared the little sparkles of light taunting her eyesight. She knew if she didn't try to calm herself, there was a good chance she'd faint. She didn't want to think about what he had to say to her. Was he going to tell her he only saw her as a friend?

They both continued until they reached his wagon nestled

off in a secluded corner where they could still see and hear the celebration around the campfire, but the noise had faded. Cora's heart raced, and her stomach twisted upon itself.

A smaller campfire was burning near his wagon, and he pointed toward a log he'd collected to sit on. "Please, have a seat," he said.

As her rump slid against the bark, her dress was tugged tight against her legs, and she shifted her weight, pulling it free. A few of the seams strained but didn't break.

"It's a nice night," he said. "Isn't it?"

"Yes. The moon is bright tonight. I always like nights with bright moons. It doesn't feel so dark when it is shining down on . . ." She let her voice trail off while the voice inside her mind screamed. Was she seriously talking about how it wasn't so dark when there was a full moon?

"Yeah. I like it too when the moon is full." He paused, glancing at her, then looking away and repeating the motion a few times. An awkward smile inched across his face. "Did you go into the fort today?"

She shook her head. "No. Harper and Grace did. But you already knew that since you saw them. I was helping Winona set up camp when Lark came to get us about Mrs. Schneider. I thought about going to see it tomorrow. I can imagine it's like Fort Kearney, though."

"Yeah, it is. It's just military barracks and supply tents."

"I did want to see if there were any women's clothes I could buy. I'd like to have a few more dresses, so I don't have to do the washing so often." She chuckled slightly, and heat rushed to the shells of her ears.

She had never hated small talk as much as she did now.

What was going on between them, she wondered. *Was the kiss that bad?*

"Did you enjoy your time in the fort?" she asked. While she

wanted to close her eyes and pray for the earth to swallow her, she didn't. It would be too obvious if she did.

"I did." He leaned back and stuck his hand in his pocket, digging around for a moment. "In fact, I got you something."

Her blood ran cold. He got her something? What was it?

Perhaps the kiss hadn't been bad at all. Perhaps he'd liked it as much as she had, and she'd been nothing short of a fool this whole time for thinking he wanted to tell her he only saw her as a friend.

"You got me something?" She brushed her fingers against her chest, lightening her voice to just above a whisper. "What is it?"

"It's this." He turned toward her, holding up a gold band between two fingers. Firelight flecked across the precious metal, and the sight of it caused her to inhale a sharp breath. Although she wasn't standing, her knees grew weak, and her body trembled. She'd imagined a man proposing to her she didn't know how many times in her life, but no matter how she'd pictured it differently every time, none of them were even like the moment she now lived. They had all paled in comparison—even the elaborately planned ones she always imagined for fun.

Jasper moved off the log, kneeling in front of her. "I don't want to say the wrong thing," he said.

She laughed. "Nothing you could say would be wrong at this moment."

"That's good to know." He glanced down at the ring and then reached for her hand. She braced herself for the words she longed to hear, and as he looked up and opened his mouth, she fought the urge to just say yes before he even asked the question.

"Cora, I—" His eyes narrowed, and he stood, dropping her hand.

"What is it?" She rose to her feet and laid her hand on his arm. "What's wrong?"

Jasper didn't say anything. He just stared off toward the trees surrounding the camp. She looked in the same direction, catching sight of someone running back into the dense brush, vanishing.

"Who was that?" she asked, wanting the answer and fearing it.

Jasper shook his head. "We need to find Mr. Mills."

"Why? Who was that?"

"I think it was Mr. Wright."

"Are you sure?"

Jasper nodded, and Mr. Mills exhaled a deep breath, grabbing the bridge of his nose.

"All right. I'll ride into the Fort in the early morning to see if I can speak to the commanding officer and let him know of the situation."

"Do you think he'll do anything?"

"I don't know. But I will find out."

EIGHTEEN

WESTON

The sun was just peeking over the horizon as Weston rode his horse into the gates of Fort Laramie and made his way straight to the military headquarters. He wasn't sure how the commanding officer would take his visit, but he wasn't about to let the man tell him no, either.

"State your business," a soldier moved in front of Weston and stopped his horse.

"I need to speak to the colonel."

"And may I ask what it is regarding?"

Weston stared down at the man young enough to be his grandson by the looks of him. Although he knew the boy had to be at least old enough to enlist in the US Calvary, he couldn't be much older than that age, and Weston wasn't about to be told what's what by a kid. "Well, of course, you ask. But that doesn't mean I'm going to tell you."

The boy's grip tightened on Weston's horses' reins. "I'm sorry, sir, but I can't let you through until I know what this is regarding."

"It's not your business, boy."

"I'm afraid it is, sir."

Another soldier approached, glancing at Weston and then at the boy the wagon master had been talking to. This new one had a different armband around his arm. "What seems to be the problem?" the second soldier asked.

"He won't tell me why he needs to speak to Colonel Johnson."

The second one looked at Weston. "I'm afraid we can't announce you unless we know what this is regarding."

Anger bubbled in Weston's chest. "Fine. It's about a dead woman who was murdered. Does that make a difference?"

Both soldiers stared at him with their eyes wide. "I'll get the colonel at once." Before Weston could say anything, the second soldier ran off while the first just stood there, his mouth was slightly agape.

It wasn't long before Weston was asked to dismount and was led into one of the main offices of the fort, and as he walked in, another man stood from behind a desk in the center of the room. It was the only piece of furniture aside from three chairs, one on one side and two on the other.

"Good morning," the colonel said. He outstretched his hand, shaking Weston's. "I'm Colonel Johnson."

"Good morning. Thank you for seeing me this morning. My name is Weston Mills. I'm a wagon master for a wagon train camped outside the fort."

"Yes, well, you should know I'm not too happy being woken at this ungodly hour." The colonel scowled. "But I was told your visit is of the utmost importance, so what can I do for you, Mr. Mills?"

"I understand, Sir, and I'm sorry to disturb you, Colonel. But this is a matter of a murdered woman and a man still on the loose. I thought you would want to know, and I've come to see if the unit stationed here can help capture the man."

The colonel's eyes widened in surprise. "A murder? Who did it?"

"His name is Sam Wright. He was a member on my train and he murdered another man's wife, Mrs. Fairchild. We don't know for sure where he is, sir. But we have reason to believe that he could have headed to this fort after fleeing our camp."

The colonel raised an eyebrow. "And why do you think that?"

"Well, he could have gone back East, but there is another woman on the wagon train that I suspect he might be after. Not to mention, he doesn't have any supplies. This fort is closer than anything he could reach if he headed back to Missouri without provisions."

The colonel rubbed his chin thoughtfully for a moment, then shook his head. "I'm sorry, Mills, but I can't do anything about this. We have no jurisdiction over what happens in your wagon train. You'll have to take care of this yourself."

"But sir," Mr. Mills protested, "if this man is a murderer, he needs to be brought to justice."

"I understand that, Mr. Mills," the colonel said, his voice firm. "But we have our own problems to deal with here at the fort. The unit that is stationed here protects the fort, not everyone passing through on random wagon trains. That would be chaos. Our jurisdiction is the fort. If this man killed the woman in the fort, then we could do something, but out in the hills of Wyoming . . . you need a Pinkerton. We can't get involved in every little dispute that happens on the trail."

A growl vibrated through Weston's chest. "I never thought I would see the day a military man wouldn't help. I suppose I shouldn't be surprised," he said curtly, turning away from the desk. "Well, thank you for your time, sir. I'll be on my way."

The colonel said nothing and instead watched as Mr. Mills turned and left, his boots clomping heavily on the wooden floor.

As Mr. Mills walked out of the commanding officer's quarters, his mind was racing with thoughts of how to handle the situation. The colonel's words echoed in his mind, emphasizing that this was a military fort, not a law enforcement agency like the Pinkerton's. They had their own responsibilities to protect the fort, not to meddle in the affairs of a wagon train.

"Darn it," Mr. Mills muttered to himself with a slight groan in his voice. "We're on our own."

He knew that he couldn't rely on the fort's soldiers to solve their problem. It was up to him and the members of the wagon train to ensure their safety. As he made his way back to his horse, his determination grew stronger. He would find a way to handle the situation without risking anyone's life, but if he came face to face with Mr. Wright, he would not hesitate to take the man down. He just needed a plan.

JASPER

Jasper lay in the grass as the darkness of the night sky faded into a light grey. Dawn would soon come, and with it, the sun and the start of a new day. He'd been up most of the night, tossing and turning as he lay just outside Cora's wagon.

He couldn't deny there'd been a time or two where he'd questioned himself, asking if he really saw whom he thought he did or if he'd just thought he saw Mr. Wright because the man had been on his mind for the last few weeks. He didn't want to think he'd been wrong, but it was also dark, and he was nervous about proposing to Cora.

He sat up, letting the blanket covering him fall to his waist as he glanced over at the wagon. Winona and the three women were asleep inside, and aside from the soft snores of the men in the grass around him and the chirps of the crickets, it was quiet.

Usually, Jasper loved this time of day for the stillness around him. There was always a calm that came with the early morning. Perhaps it was just because most people were still asleep, blissfully dreaming while he enjoyed the world around him alone. Although, he supposed it really didn't matter. Calm was calm, and he would take every second of it he could—especially now.

Today was supposed to be a different type of day. Today was supposed to be the start of a new life with Cora. A day when they would tell everyone of their plans to marry and talk to the preacher about marrying them. Perhaps they even would have just married today—or this evening—not wanting to waste any time. Why wait? He had thought all afternoon yesterday after buying the ring.

But now it was filled with this gut-twisting feeling that Jasper hadn't seen the last of Mr. Wright.

Jasper rose to his feet, stretching the sleepiness from his muscles before making his way over to the fire. Although the soreness in his shoulder had faded, he still kept his arm wrapped around his body to limit movement. He hated having it tied down. It made him feel broken. He knelt in front of the dying flames and grabbed a nearby stick, poking at the chunks of burnt wood in an effort to reposition them and give the fire a bit of kindling to reignite. It worked slightly, and the flames grew again, sending bits of ash into the air, where they floated back down to the ground and extinguished. He watched the fire until the sun started turning the cloudless grey sky into bright shades of orange and yellow.

Sounds rustled from the wagon, and as Jasper looked up, Cora slipped from the bonnet, stepping down to the grass. She looked at him, and her eyes widened for a second.

"I'm sorry to scare you," he whispered.

"It's all right."

"Can you not sleep?"

She shook her head. "No. You?"

"Not really." He motioned toward the fire. "Care to have a seat?"

She nodded, following him to the campfire and sitting beside him. "That was quite the interesting night last night, wasn't it?" she asked. Although she had a slight chuckle to her breath, he got the feeling that she didn't find anything about what she said amusing.

"Yeah. Unfortunately, it was." He paused, looking out onto the horizon. "I was just thinking how it didn't end as I thought it would."

"Neither did I. Although, my expectations were vastly different from yours. Or at least they were when I started the night."

"I wish it hadn't turned out the way it did."

"Me too."

He inhaled another deep breath as the question sitting on the tip of his tongue mocked him. Certainly, now wouldn't be the right time to finish what he'd started, but at the same time, he didn't want to risk losing the chance. What if because he waited in asking, she would have time to realize that she didn't love him enough to marry him?

He cleared his throat. "About last night. I . . . I didn't get a chance to finish what I wanted to say to you." His stomach twisted upon itself, and his heart raced. He could feel sweat bubbling on the back of his neck, and his voice lightened in a funny tone that cracked. "I don't know how you're feeling about it, but—"

"Yes. Yes, is how I'm feeling."

He sucked in a breath. "Yes to my question? Yes, you'll marry me?"

She nodded and reached for his hand, clutching it in hers. "Yes, I'll marry you."

He jumped to his feet, tugging her along with him, and after he wiggled his hand from hers, he wrapped his good arm around her, hugging her tight. His mother had told him he didn't know how many times that when he'd find the right woman, he would know. He hadn't really believed her until now, and so much of him wished his parents were there so they could meet Cora.

One day, he thought, *perhaps I'll see them again, and they can meet my wife.*

He stepped back from Cora, digging in his pocket and pulling out the ring once more. "It's not much, but it's all I have now, and I will get you a better one when we reach Oregon."

"You don't have to. This one is perfect."

She looked down, watching as he slipped the ring on her finger. Tears misted her eyes, and as he leaned in to kiss her, she mimicked his movement kissing him in return.

Footsteps thumped in the grass behind them, and as Jasper jerked away and spun, he drew the gun from the holster around his waist and pointed it. He was never a great shot with his left arm, but if he had to, he'd use it anyway. Mr. Mills emerged from the bright light, holding up his hands. "Don't go drawing a weapon. It's just me," he said. A slight chuckle whispered through his words.

"If you don't want a gun pointing at you, perhaps you shouldn't sneak up on people so early in the morning."

"Well, I didn't think anyone would be awake."

Jasper snorted. "And that is probably even a worse time to approach someone else's wagon."

"You know, you're probably right. I'll rethink my choices next time." Mr. Mills removed his hat and wiped his forehead, letting out a deep, sighing breath. He nodded to Cora. "Miss Randall."

"Good morning," she said to him.

"Did you speak to the commanding officer of the fort?" Jasper asked.

"I did. And let me tell you; he was not too happy with me

waking him up." Mr. Mills cast Jasper a sideways glance as he rested his hands on his hips. "Have you got any coffee made?"

Jasper shook his head, and although he wanted to tell the wagon master to forget the coffee and tell him what the officer said, he didn't. Instead, he went to the task of filling up a kettle and hooking it on the fire. Cora helped where she could.

"So, what did the officer say?" Jasper asked the wagon master.

"He wants us to leave."

"What? Why?" Jasper furrowed his brow. "Is he not going to help us?"

"No. He's not. The only thing we can do is either take this up with the Pinkertons when we reach Oregon or deal with the man ourselves."

"And how are we supposed to do that?"

"The only thing I can think of is we leave the fort and see if he is following us."

"So we're just supposed to leave?"

"Yeah."

"But what about Mrs. Schneider? I thought she would have a few days' rest before we leave."

"Unfortunately, I won't be able to give her that. She's going to be ready to leave in the morning. We all will."

Jasper sucked in a breath and wiped his whole face with one hand. His brow furrowed. "I don't like this plan. I don't like leaving the safety of the fort."

"I don't care for it much either, but it's all we can do."

Jasper looked at Cora. "Do you know how to shoot a gun?" he asked her.

She shook her head.

"Well, that's something we will have to fix."

CORA

Cora hadn't ever seen a gun, much less held one or shot one. It wasn't that she hated them or didn't want to be near them; it was just that living at the orphanage wasn't exactly a place she—or anyone living there—would need one.

Looking down at Jasper's pistol, though, her stomach churned, and her throat tightened. In her mind, guns had always been a tool for hunting and a source to get food. Sure, she knew they were always for protection too, but it wasn't until this moment that she felt the magnitude of what she was about to do. Those who wheeled the guns took lives—whether human or animal.

"Are you ready?" Jasper stood in front of her, holding the gun in his hand.

She looked over to Grace and Harper, who were standing with her. They, too, needed to learn while Lark and Winona stood off to the side. Those two had already learned how to handle a pistol. The two watched, chatting in whispers that Cora couldn't hear.

"Um, I think so."

As she reached for the gun, he yanked it away, spun it around on his finger, pointed it, and fired. The meadow had been quiet, peaceful, and serene and was abruptly interrupted by a loud gunshot. All three women slapped their hands over their ears, and Grace closed her eyes, slightly screaming.

The thunderous shot pounded through Cora's chest, and wildlife fled the trees around the meadow, just as scared as she was.

"Why did you do that?" she yelled at him,

"I just wanted to make sure you were paying attention." He held out the gun again. "Take it."

"Are you going to tease me again?"

He chuckled and shook his head. "I won't. I promise."

The hair on her arms stood, and her stomach churned with the thought of the task at hand. Exactly what about her screamed that she'd want to do such things, she didn't know. "Why do I have to do this again?" she asked.

"Because I need you to be able to protect yourself. I can't always be with you, and I don't want anything to happen to you."

"I don't know if I can do this."

"Of course, you can, and I will teach you. Do you see the targets?" he said, pointing North about twenty yards from where they stood.

"I suppose so. Do you really expect me to hit those?"

He ignored her question and grabbed her hand, setting the gun in her palm. His calmness annoyed her about as much as his confidence in her ability. How could he be so calm? And how could he think she could do this?

"Everyone should know how to shoot a gun, Cora—especially the one I plan to marry."

Harper and Grace both gasped and looked at one another. Cora glanced over her shoulder at them, giving them a slight nod.

"Now, do you want to know how it works?"

Before she could answer, he moved close to her and began explaining the technique. His voice purred while his fingers glided over the steel barrel and down the handle, and he pointed at different parts, describing them before he showed her how to stand and brace herself. To her horror, within moments of his starting his lesson, the gun rested in her slippery hands, pointing at one of the targets.

"All right. You're ready. Pull the trigger."

Inhaling a deep protecting breath, she closed her eyes and bent her finger. The gun exploded in her hand, sending vibrations through her whole body. The force of the weapon firing knocked her off balance, and she took several steps backward.

Her shoe caught on a massive chunk of grass, and she slipped. Her rump hit the ground.

Grace and Harper gasped again, and Jasper lunged toward her, dropping to his knees. "Are you all right?"

She chuckled slightly. "I think so."

"Do you think you can do it again?"

"Do I have a choice?"

He shook his head. "Not really. No."

"All right."

She shot several more times, and before he motioned that it was Harper's turn, he took her out to the log target to show her where the bullets had bit the bark. Only two marks greeted them, while the rest of her shots hadn't been close enough at all to do any damage.

"Your aim is horrible," he laughed.

She cocked her head to the side. "How nice of you to mock your future wife."

"You know, aside from your tone, I rather like hearing those words." He leaned in, and although he hinted at a kiss on her lips, catching sight of Winona, who was watching them, Cora wasn't surprised he kissed her forehead instead.

NINETEEN

CORA

The early morning hours came before Cora could even think about them or what they would bring for the day. Everyone on the wagon train had been packed and ready, and when Mr. Mills gave the signal, they all moved out, following him down the trail and away from Fort Laramie. Cora glanced over her shoulder a few times, watching as the fort vanished from her sight in the distance. Their once safe haven was now gone; she couldn't help but feel as though they were now at the mercy of fate.

And the fear of the unknown formed knots in her stomach.

While she had planned on riding in the wagon with Winona and the other women, Jasper had requested she ride with him, and as the wagon rolled down the trail, her body swayed from side to side, knocking into his from time to time. Their shoulders bumped, and each time he would smile.

They rode for most of the day in silence. Only chatting about things here and there that held no depth or meaning. Just the mundane topics that required no thought or effort while they stayed away from the one thing they both knew they should talk about but couldn't—Sam Wright. Cora couldn't help but feel a sense of guilt about the whole situation. She had never intended to fall for Sam, but her heart had taken control of her mind. It was a foolish mistake and one she wished she could change.

Perhaps it was her guilt that kept her so quiet, for it wasn't until they had stopped and set up camp for the night that either of them spoke.

"I've got to fetch some water from the river, and I don't want to leave you here alone," Jasper said, grabbing a bucket and holding it out. "So, do you want to come with me?"

"Are you asking or telling?" she chuckled.

"I suppose telling. I just didn't want to sound like it."

"It's all right, you know." She moved toward him, leaning in so her face was inches from his. "I know you aren't telling me because you're a vile man who likes to control a woman's every move." She wiggled her eyebrows, and he laughed.

She took the bucket from him, and he grabbed another, hooking the handle around his arm. He clenched his teeth at his inability to move his other arm, and his brow furrowed.

"I think I'm going to take this off today," he said.

"Do you think you should?" She reached out, letting her fingers trace along the material wrapped over his shoulder and down around his arm.

"I can always ask Dr. Evans. But it's not really sore anymore. I could always try and see. You know, take it off, and if it bothers me, put it back on."

"You could. I guess it's something to think about." She followed him away from the wagon down a pathway through the grass to the river, glancing over her shoulder toward the camp. She saw Winona and the other women setting up their camp, and she paused, watching them for a second before continuing to follow Jasper toward the river with the buckets swinging lightly by her side.

The camp was nestled in a picturesque spot, surrounded by

rolling hills and framed by the grove of trees lining the riverbank. While Cora had loved Nebraska, Wyoming was a whole other type of prairie, and as they neared the river, the water sparkled under the sun's gentle rays, casting a serene aura over the entire scene.

Cora dipped her bucket into the cool water, her eyes never leaving the breathtaking view. "It's pretty here," she said.

"Yeah. It is." He dunked his own bucket in the water, watching it fill. "I think it will only get more pretty the closer we get to California and Oregon."

She glanced over at him. She hadn't thought much about their destination as the last few days had been full of so many other distractions. She chewed on the side of her cheek. "About California . . ." She let her voice trail off, unsure of what she wanted to say.

"Yes?" He raised one eyebrow and smiled as though he knew where she wanted to go with her questions even though she didn't.

The truth of it was that it wasn't about California or Oregon. She knew that she would have to go with her husband where he chose to go. The thought of leaving Winona, however, caused a knot in her throat, and it dropped to the pit of her stomach, rolling around like a rock. She'd been with her headmistress for pretty much her whole life.

"Of course, I will follow you," she finally said. "I just . . . it's hard to think about leaving Winona."

"I understand. I felt the same way about leaving my family."

"But you did."

"Yeah, I did."

"Do you think you will ever see them again?"

"I don't know. I would like to say yes, but I don't know. I have thought about a few years down the road, like after I have some money and a family, perhaps I could travel back home so they can meet my wife and children. But just because

I can dream it or picture it in my mind doesn't mean it will happen."

"Perhaps it will. Perhaps the train will expand West, or you'll find that you want to go home no matter what the journey entails."

"Do you mean *we* will find *we* will want to go home?" He glanced at her, smiling. "It would be a great honor to introduce you to them."

"And it would be a great honor to meet them."

He studied her for a moment, cocking his head to the side. "How about we make a deal about California?"

"What is the deal?"

"How about we decide what we will do when we reach Fort Hall?"

"I think that is a good deal."

"So, about us getting married. When did you want to talk to the preacher?" Jasper lifted the bucket out of the water and set it on the small sandy beach. He glanced from the bucket to her, stretching his shoulders as though the wrapped one was bothering him.

She shrugged. "I don't know. Perhaps today."

"If we talked to him today, we could maybe be married by tonight."

Her heart thumped with the thought of tonight. Of course, it had been everything she had ever dreamed and wanted, and it was close enough that she could taste it. Being married. Having a husband. Being a wife.

It was everything.

And yet she couldn't help but fear it too, at least until they didn't have to worry about Sam. "Do you think we should wait until we know Mr. Wright is no longer following us?" As soon as she asked, part of her regretted it.

"We could. If you wanted." Jasper gave her a sideways glance.

A slight sadness hitched in not only his eyes but the tone of his voice.

"It's not that I want to. I don't know. Perhaps it was foolish of me to even say."

"It's not foolish. I understand how you feel, and I'll respect your choice."

They both stood, and Cora glanced back toward the camp set off in the distance. She could only see the tops of the wagon bonnets poking through the trees and tall grass.

A crack echoed in the air, and Cora turned to see Sam standing menacingly behind Jasper, a gun held tightly in his grasp. Jasper's eyes widened, and he crumpled to the ground, unconscious after Sam struck him in the back of the head with the butt of the gun.

"Jasper!" Cora cried out, her voice filled with panic and anguish. She rushed to his side and dropped to her knees beside him, trembling as she looked up at Sam. "What have you done? Why are you doing this?"

Sam sneered. His eyes were fixed on her, and his face twisted into a malicious grin. He towered over her. "I did what I should have done a long time ago."

Tears brimmed her eyes and streamed down her cheeks. She cradled Jasper's head in her lap, whispering the prayer that he was still alive.

"Course," Sam continued, waving toward her. "I suppose it wouldn't have mattered if I had. It looks like you've made your choice. Too bad it's the wrong one. I guess now you'll also have to pay for it."

"Pay for it?"

"You should have picked me. We could have had a good life together." He paused, inhaling a deep breath. "I suppose we still can. Get up. You're coming with me, and we're going to leave the wagon train like we should have. We are going to be together like we should have."

Cora's gaze blazed with defiance. "I am not going anywhere with you."

Sam's rage intensified, and he spat out his words venomously. "You think you're above me, don't you? Let me tell you something, Cora. That woman who died, it's because of you. If Mrs. Fairchild hadn't made you fall in front of that snake, Mr. Scott wouldn't have saved you, and I wouldn't have had to punish her. It's all because of you. You are to blame for it all. I was merely the man to do the job that needed to be done in order to keep us together and you safe."

Cora's hands trembled as she held them up in a futile attempt to reason with Sam. "That's not true. I never asked for any of this. You're responsible for your own actions. You killed Mrs. Fairchild. It's no one's fault but your own."

Sam's eyes narrowed, and his gaze fell upon the gold band on Cora's ring finger. His face contorted with a mixture of jealousy and anger. "Engaged, are you? To that weakling on the ground? Do you think you can replace me so easily?"

Cora's voice wavered but held a fierce determination. "Jasper is a good man. He never would have killed a woman . . . not for any reason. He loves me, and I love him. Nothing you say or do will change that."

Without warning, Sam lunged toward Cora, and she jumped to her feet, trying to back away from him. Her shoes pressed into the sand, making deep impressions. She tried to scream, but before she could, Sam's hands closed around her throat. She gasped for breath, her eyes widening in terror. The world around her dimmed with darkness as Sam's grip tightened.

Before Cora's vision could fade completely, she caught sight of Jasper opening his eyes. He blinked several times, looking at her before he sat up and shook his head. The scene before him seemed to register in his mind, and a surge of strength and willpower jolted through him. He seemed to fight through the haze, and he reached for his gun holstered at his waist. In a desperate act of protection, he aimed and fired, the bullet grazing Sam's arm.

Sam released his hold on Cora, cursing in pain as he stumbled backward.

"You don't know the trouble you have just caused yourself," Sam said.

"Yeah, well, considering you're about to meet our maker, I don't really care."

"This isn't the end of me." Sam laughed, tapping the side of his temple and then pointing toward Cora. "I'll be back for her. I will always come back for her."

"You won't come near her ever again." Jasper cocked the gun again, and Sam darted for the trees, fleeing into the wilderness. Although Jasper couldn't be sure, he thought he'd heard Sam saying something about seeing him again.

Cora crumpled to the ground, gasping for air and clutching her neck. Jasper rushed to her side, struggling through the sand. His eyes were wide with concern, and he knelt beside her, taking her into his arms and pulling her close. She buried her face into his chest, sobbing uncontrollably. Jasper held her tightly and ran his fingers through her hair, trying to soothe her.

"It's all right," he whispered. "I've got you. You're safe. You're safe."

~

The sound of approaching footsteps broke through the stillness, and members of the wagon train rushed to the scene, their faces etched with concern. Mr. Mills was the first to make it to them.

"It was Mr. Wright. He ran off that way through the trees," Jasper said to the wagon master.

Mr. Mills signaled to the rest of the men, who darted back to the wagons to gather their horses and ride off after the criminal.

Jasper squinted as though his head throbbed with pain, and he cradled her in his arms as best as he could. "Are you all right?" He asked her.

With tears streaming down her face, she managed to nod weakly. "I'll be fine."

Relief seemed to flood through his face, and she clung to him, burying her face in his chest again. He kissed the top of her head.

"Do you think he'll come back?" she asked.

He wanted to tell her no, and that Sam was gone for good, but he couldn't. Even if he didn't know much about the man, he knew the difference between a promise and a threat. Threats often become forgotten, said in a moment of anger and frustration when the person wants to sound as though they would do another harm. But what Mr. Wright said and the way he said it, his words weren't empty. They were a promise.

He would be back.

And he would return for Cora.

"I don't know. Maybe."

She pulled away from Jasper, looking into his eyes. "Do you remember when I said I thought perhaps we should wait to marry?" she asked.

"Yeah." His voice was a breathless whisper.

"I don't want to wait anymore. I want to get married as soon as the pastor will do it."

TWENTY

CORA

The sun hung low in the sky, casting long shadows over the wagons circled around the campsite. In the dimly lit corner near the back of Winona's wagon, Cora stood in a clean dress with a bushel of wildflowers tucked in her hair behind one ear. Her fingers nervously traced the frayed edges of her sleeve. The dress had seen better days, but it was still the one that she'd picked to get married in.

She looked out at the campsite, and she could see families gathered around their own fires, children running around, and the sounds of laughter and chatter. Her breath was heavy with a touch of anticipation as Winona walked around her, adjusting her hair before fixing a wayward button that hadn't been buttoned properly.

"I don't think I can help you look any more perfect than you already do," the headmistress said.

"Thank you for your help." She looked at Harper and Grace, standing a few feet from them. "And thank you both too."

They smiled.

She glanced down at her hands, watching them tremble as she fidgeted with her fingers. "We had thought about waiting because of Mr. Wright. But I decided I didn't want to. I just hope I'm not making a mistake."

"Why would you think that?" Winona asked. The headmistress's eyes flickered with a hint of concern while defiance washed over her features. "Marrying Jasper is a fine thing, Cora. Of course, you don't want to ignore the dangers lurking around us, but don't let it bother you, either."

Cora shrugged. "I don't know. Perhaps I'm just being foolish."

"You aren't being foolish," a voice said behind her. She turned to see Lark approaching. Although she smiled, there was a distant look to her. Her skin was pale, and she looked like she didn't feel well. "Besides, no one here will let a man scare us off." She scoffed, her voice dripping with defiance. "You shouldn't let someone else dictate your own happiness, Cora. If he makes you happy and you want to get married, then you should, and you shouldn't concern yourself with what anyone else thinks."

Cora took a deep breath, trying to steady her nerves. "I appreciate your kind words."

"You're welcome. And I mean them. No matter what has ever happened between us, I'm happy for you." Lark opened her arms, hugging Cora, and as she pulled away, Lark's face twisted. She spun on her heels and darted away from the wagon, bending over to wretch whatever she had for supper.

Harper and Grace rushed to her, laying their hands on her back. "Lark? Are you all right?" Harper asked. She glanced at Winona, who hadn't moved from Cora's side. "Aren't you going to help her? What's wrong with her?"

"Nothing is wrong with her," Winona said.

Lark wiped her mouth, and her voice trembled as her gaze cast downward. "I'm all right. It's nothing to worry yourselves about."

"Nothing to worry about? Lark, you just lost your supper. Are you sick?"

"In a manner of speaking, but it's all right, and you don't have to be concerned."

Harper and Grace exchanged glances, and as they looked at Winona, the notion of what they were missing hit Cora like an arrow to a target.

"Lark is having a baby!" Cora shouted.

The two women slapped their hands over their mouths and looked at Lark. Tears welled up in the young woman's eyes as she nodded, saying nothing as though she was unable to find her voice. The air between all the women fell into a hushed silence, the weight of Lark's revelation settling over them like a fragile web of emotions.

It wasn't just Winona and the four women anymore.

Two of them were married.

And now there would be a baby.

Harper sucked in a breath, and she lunged for Lark, wrapping her arms around her neck in a tight hug. "Well, isn't that something? Congratulations, Lark."

Lark's lips quivered, a mixture of relief and vulnerability on her face. "Thanks," she murmured, her voice barely audible.

Cora didn't know if it was the look on Lark's face, the sound of her voice, or the fact that Cora's own emotions were on a rollercoaster from not only the problems with Sam but her newfound love with Jasper and the fact that she was getting married in mere moments. But in that second, looking upon the woman as she rubbed her forehead and looked like she could get sick any second, Cora's heart swelled with compassion. Her worries were momentarily overshadowed, and she made her way to Lark, reaching for the young woman's hand in a gesture of friendship.

"Congratulations," Cora whispered.

"Thank you."

Winona moved to the two women, rubbing her hands down

both of their arms. "While I love seeing you all together like this, I think it's time for a wedding, don't you?" she asked.

All four women nodded.

~

The early evening sun cast a golden hue over the sprawling tall grass, and its rays gently warmed the earth as Cora made her way toward the river—the perfect place for her and Jasper to marry. Dappled sunlight filtered through the canopy of trees, and as Jasper turned to face Cora, his eyes brimmed with affection.

He reached out, grabbing her hand. Her nimble fingers entwined with his calloused ones, and they turned to Preacher Levinson and smiled.

"Friends, we have gathered today in this beautiful spot near the river to watch as our fellow companions, Mr. Jasper Scott and Miss Cora Randall, join in holy matrimony. Love is a sacred bond, a flame that flickers through the ages, and today we celebrate the beginning of their shared journey." He opened his Bible and turned to Jasper. "Jasper, do you take Cora to be your lawfully wedded wife, to have and to hold, from this day forward? Do you also promise to cherish and protect her and to love her in joys and sorrows until the end of your days?"

"I do," Jasper said. His voice was full of resolute and love, and he gazed into Cora's eyes, his fingers gently squeezing hers.

"And, Cora, do you take Jasper to be your lawfully wedded husband to have and to hold from this day forward? Do you also promise to cherish and protect him and to love him in joys and sorrows until the end of your days?"

Cora's heart swelled with joy as tears shimmered in her eyes. "I do," she whispered. Her voice trembled with emotion as she looked into Jasper's eyes.

Preacher Levinson smiled as his voice carried over the

crowd. "Jasper and Cora, you have declared your love and commitment before these witnesses. May your bond grow stronger with each passing day, and may your love endure the test of time. By the power vested in me, I now pronounce you husband and wife. You may seal your vows with a kiss."

Jasper and Cora leaned toward each other, and their lips met in a tender kiss.

They were now husband and wife.

They were now married.

TWENTY-ONE

WINONA

The first rays of dawn peeked through the wagon's bonnet, casting a soft glow on Winona's face. As she opened her eyes, a smile inched across her lips. While there was plenty to do this morning before the wagon train left camp, she couldn't help but feel the joy of knowing that two of the young women had found love and marriage.

One even had the precious gift of new life growing inside her.

It was all Winona had wanted for all four women, and while she had been confident when they left Missouri that her dreams for them would all come true, she hadn't expected it to happen so fast.

With a contented sigh, Winona rose from her makeshift bed and donned one of her worn but cherished dresses. She didn't know how much longer she could wear it, but she was determined to get every last day out of the fabric she could. She climbed down from the wagon and surveyed the camp, the vibrant energy of everyone starting to prepare breakfast while also packing their wagons bustled around her. Her gaze fell upon the campfire where Grace and Harper sat side by side, their smiles radiant as they chatted animatedly with one another.

"Good morning, Winona." Grace's melodious voice rang out.

"Good morning, ladies. I'm sorry I slept in."

"You don't have to apologize. We wanted you to. That's why we didn't wake you." Harper glanced at Grace, then threw a few strips of bacon in the hot pan sitting on the fire. The meat sizzled and scrunched up while the fat started to render.

"We have breakfast almost finished," Grace said, pointing toward a few slices of bread sitting on a few plates. "It's not much, but it will fill the stomach this morning."

"It looks and smells good, and that's all that matters. Once we are finished, we can pack the rest of the supplies. I want to be ready when Mr. Mills wants to leave."

The three women settled around the campfire. Chatting about the wedding and the baby and how much had changed in the months after leaving Missouri while the breakfast continued to cook. While she partook in the conversation, Winona couldn't help but sit back and watch, more often than not, enjoying the banter between the two women as they talked of the trip so far. Her heart swelled with a hint of pride as she watched them seem to flourish against the backdrop of the frontier.

Harper, with her strong and ever-practical side, had taken everything in just as she always had, living her days as the characters in the books she so loved. She deserved someone who would embrace her nose-stuck-in-a-book nature and challenge her every day, even through the trials that lay ahead.

And then there was Grace, with her gentle nature and soft-spoken heart, who had come out of the shell she'd clung to for so many years. Even though she still was quiet, there was a difference to her, and she deserved to find a love that matched her kindness.

Winona's thoughts turned to the eligible bachelors on the

wagon train. Of course, love couldn't be forced, but she couldn't help but wonder if any of them held the key to the women's happiness.

Two down, two to go, she thought to herself. *Two down, two to go.*

HER OREGON TRAIL BLACKSMITH

Four orphans and their headmistress set out for Oregon in search of men looking for mail-order brides. Will they find what they are looking for? Or will fate have other plans?

Order the series today or Read for FREE with Kindle Unlimited

Turn the page for a sneak peek at book two, Her Oregon Trail Blacksmith.

ONE

WINONA

As the sun rose over the vast expanse of the Wyoming landscape, Winona found herself immersed in a symphony of colors and scents, surrounded by the beauty of nature. Venturing into the wild, undulating fields, her fingers yearned to pluck the ripe berries hidden amidst the foliage.

It had become one of her favorite pastimes while on the wagon train, and although she wanted to share it with the other women, she also enjoyed the time alone. It was something she could do without the constant chatter of others around her.

With each step, the soft crunch of the grass beneath her feet whispered secrets of the land while the gentle breeze teased her hair, carrying the sweet fragrance of wildflowers and the earthy scent of the fertile soil. Along with the morning scents, the vibrant blue sky stretched endlessly above her, a canvas upon which nature painted its masterpiece, and as she wandered through the verdant tapestry, Winona couldn't help but feel a profound connection to the land. It was as if the spirit of Wyoming itself embraced her, whispering stories and secrets that only she would know about.

Although Wyoming had proved more of the same prairie

plains of Nebraska, there was a difference to them, and she knew she would miss them once they crossed over into Montana and continued into Idaho and Oregon—or whatever the country Mr. Mills said they would pass through. She wasn't paying much attention to him at the time, and while part of her regretted it, the bigger part didn't. Annoying to a fault, Mr. Mills sure knew how to push her buttons and get on her every last nerve. She didn't know how someone could be as frustrating and stubborn as the wagon master. Surely, there was no one else like him, and she'll never know how she had managed to cross his path. She rolled her eyes as she thought of all the arguments they'd had. One thing was certain: the day they arrived in Oregon and went their separate ways would be the happiest day in her life.

Continuing through the trees near the river, she stumbled upon several berry bushes, and she studied the leaves and plumpness of precious gems of fruit nestled among the thorny stems. Bending down, her fingers caressed the leaves as she carefully plucked each berry. Their vivid hues stained her fingertips with a hint of crimson and indigo, and she licked the juices off, tasting the sweetness mixed with a bit of sourness.

If she only had an oven to make a pie...

The sound of leaves rustled behind her, and as she stood and turned, Mrs. Stonemill and Mrs. Reed emerged from the bushes with baskets in their arms. Their eyes widened, and Mrs. Reed sucked in a breath.

"Oh. Miss Callahan, we didn't expect to find anyone here." Mrs. Stonemill bushed her hand against her chest. Her words were more like breathless syllables on her lips than anything. Oozing with a little shock before her shoulders seemed to relax.

"I'm sorry if I startled you," Winona said. "I thought I would find some berries this morning for the women to enjoy with breakfast."

"We thought the same thing. Unfortunately, it's been a while since we've found any we want to trust enough to eat."

The two women moved toward the berry bush, looking at the fruit for a moment before they, too, plucked the gems from the leaves and stems.

"But these look lovely."

"They seem to be. I tried to study a few books before we left on the poisonous ones. But sometimes, details get fuzzy in my head. I should have brought Harper with me. She knows more about them than I do. But that's usually the case with her. She's so smart, and she loves to learn."

"And is Harper, Miss McCall or Miss Linwell?" Mrs. Reed asked, pausing on a particularly hard berry she crushed while trying to free it from the stem. She licked the juice off her finger and thumb, making a slight face at the tartness.

"Miss McCall. She has always been the bookworm of the four women. She was always the most interested in her studies and schooling, and as she got older, she helped me teach the younger ones. In fact, she would like to become a teacher when we get to Oregon."

The two women's heads whipped toward one another's as they looked at each other. A silent conversation seemed to flow between them until Mrs. Reed nudged Mrs. Stonemill and nodded.

Mrs. Stonemill shook her head. "I'm not sure that's the best idea," she finally said.

"What's not the best idea?" Winona asked.

Mrs. Reed moved around Mrs. Stonemill, and although the latter tried to stop the other wife, Mrs. Reed ignored her.

"Well, it just so happens we were just discussing the trouble we've had with the children's education on the wagon train. It seems that all the families have been trying to teach them, but it's proving to be a challenge. We don't understand why. Perhaps it's just the nature of being out here. It's too distracting, and everyone is teaching different things. It's confusing the children. Not to mention, with everything that needs tending to on this journey... it's been difficult to give the children the attention they need. We thought if we could get them all together, perhaps they would help each other."

Nodding sympathetically, Winona set her basket down. "I understand your concern. Education is a precious gift, and every child deserves the opportunity to learn and grow no matter where they are—even if they are traveling on a wagon train." She chuckled, brushing her fingertips against her forehead."

"That is our thoughts too." Mrs. Reed looked at Mrs. Stonemill, ignoring how the latter gave her a disagreeable look as she turned back to Winona. "Do you think Miss McCall would be interested in helping teach the children?"

Before Winona could open her mouth, Mrs. Stonemill spoke. "I'm not sure that is the best idea."

"Why not?" Winona asked the woman.

"It's nothing against Miss McCall, Miss Callahan. I'm sure she is a lovely woman, but..."

"But what?"

"Well, you have to agree that one's background should be taken into consideration, especially from the parents."

"So, you're unsure because she lacks teaching credentials? Indeed, she doesn't. But she wants to obtain them when we get to Oregon, and I believe she will have no trouble doing so. She's so smart, and she loves to learn new things."

"I understand she has plans, and I'm not worried about that. It's just..." Mrs. Stonemill bit her lip for a moment. "I don't wish for this to sound rude, but well, Mrs. Evans..."

"What about Lark?"

"It's no secret around the wagon train of where she came from and what she did."

"She didn't do anything. She was just a girl when I took her from that place, and she hadn't done anything she should be ashamed of." Anger bubbled in Winona's chest, and she hardened her tone, clenching her jaw as she straightened her shoulders.

How dare this woman.

"Furthermore, may I point out that a gentleman . . . a doctor, chose Lark for his bride. Do you think he would have done so if he saw her as tarnished?" Winona raised one eyebrow, cocking her head to the side. "Because he didn't. So, I don't see where you have any cause to judge this situation. Lark's past does not define her." Winona looked at both women. "And neither would Harper's if she had one, which she does not. She was left at the orphanage by an Aunt and Uncle who couldn't care for her after her parents died. She may not have come from a prominent background, but her determination and dedication are unmatched. She believes in the transformative power of education. It's her character and her passion that matters most. She has an innate ability to connect with children, to inspire them to learn and grow, and I have seen it firsthand."

While Mrs. Reed's eyebrows rose and concern etched across her face, Mrs. Stonemill remained unreadable.

"I'm sure you have," Mrs. Reed finally said. "And I, for one, believe you." The woman looked at the other. "I think the other parents would agree with me too."

Mrs. Stonemill inhaled a deep breath and cleared her throat. "I suppose I can agree with that." She looked at Winona. "I'm sorry if I offended you. It was not my intention. I only meant to say that it's not every day we see a woman of Lark's . . . background, I suppose, joining our community. But I can understand and sympathize with the pain a young girl, who was forced into something she didn't want, felt. I'm sure it wasn't pleasant for her."

"No, it wasn't. And she was forced. Her father sold her after her mother died, leaving her to the warrants of a horrible woman. Lark had no choice, no say."

Mrs. Reed covered her mouth with her hand. "We had no idea."

"Well, that always seems to happen when you judge others without knowing the details about what happened." Winona's eyes moved from one woman to the other. Her shoulders still taunt with annoyance.

Mrs. Reed leaned toward Winona, laying a hand on her shoulder. "It is a fine testament that she did what she could to survive such a horrible situation and that she turned out to be a lovely woman. From the trip's start, I noticed how Dr. Evans was quite taken with her, and they looked happy together." Mrs. Reed smiled, and while it wasn't fake, there was a sense that her guilt over Mrs. Stonemill's behavior was causing her to exaggerate her praise of the young woman.

For a moment, Winona thought about correcting her; however, Mrs. Reed did nothing to feel bad for.

"And as for Miss McCall," Mrs. Reed continued. "I'm sure Mrs. Stonemill didn't mean anything by it, and we can all agree that she's a perfectly nice girl who, if she loves teaching, would probably be an excellent solution to our problem."

Winona nodded, still feeling irked but deciding to let it go. "I think she would be too."

"So, will you ask her for us?"

"I'd be happy to."

HARPER

"In the hallowed halls of academia and the vibrant corridors of knowledge, a profound artistry exists that transcends the mere transmission of facts and figures. It is the art of teaching, a sacred endeavor that holds within its embrace the power to shape hearts and minds, ignite the flames of curiosity, and inspire the pursuit of wisdom."

Harper looked up from the book in her hands, glancing toward the sky. The words she'd just read repeated in her mind, and as she thought about each one, she tried to memorize it in her soul. She'd always felt that to love teaching was to embark on a timeless journey, guided by the light of knowledge and fueled by an insatiable thirst to share the beauty and intricacies of the world with eager souls yearning to learn. But the more she thought about it, that little definition almost seemed not enough to describe how one could witness the marvel of transformation as ignorance gave way to understanding, confusion to clarity, and hesitation to confidence.

That was perhaps what she loved the most.

She loved seeing how a child's eyes lit up when they realized they could use their mind to explore the world.

So many times, she would help the children at the orphanage, and she always had this sense that each interaction was a symphony where each lesson was a carefully composed melody resonating through the chambers of receptive minds. It was a dance of inspiration, where she—the teacher—became both a conductor and a participant, guiding the rhythm of learning while also being swept away by the joy of discovery.

"Daydreaming again?" she heard a voice ask.

It jarred her attention, and she looked toward Winona, who approached her with two buckets in the headmistress's hands.

Harper knew what that meant—chores.

"It's not daydreaming," she said. "I was just thinking."

"Let me guess... teaching."

"You know me well."

"Well, it was always the only thing you wanted to do each day. I swear, sometimes I wondered if you would make the children do lessons every day without a break. I think at times they feared it too." Winona laughed as she sat in the grass next to Harper and adjusted her skirt around her legs.

"To be honest, I wanted to. But I also know that working all the time only brings disinterest, and I never wanted to bore them or sway them away from learning."

"I don't think you would have done that. You always had a way of educating them when they didn't even know it."

"Well, education is not merely confined to textbooks and classrooms. In fact, I think it's best when they aren't. It's usually when they don't know they are learning that they ask the most profound questions and seek meaningful answers."

Winona shook her head. "That is far too much thought for me. Even if I believe education is important, I have never looked at it through the depth you do."

This wasn't the first time Harper had heard these words from her headmistress. In fact, Winona had said it a dozen times before—perhaps even two. For the longest time, Harper wondered if something was wrong with her thinking. Was it wrong to want to ignite a flame within young hearts, fueling the fires of ambition and illuminating the limitless possibilities that lie ahead?

Harper didn't think so.

She'd always thought that in the hands of a passionate educator, a classroom became a sanctuary where knowledge is not bestowed but shared, where wisdom is not imposed but discovered. To teach is to become an architect of dreams, constructing the foundations upon which the aspirations of future generations shall rest. She'd once read, and the words had stuck with her ever since.

"Do you think it's bad that I do that?" she asked, biting her lip as though she wasn't sure if she was ready for the answer.

"Oh, heaven's no, child. I have never thought that."

"You've said so many times I figured you did."

"Not once. It's far more commendable than not." Winona hesitated a moment and inhaled a deep breath. "It just makes me wonder about what you want in life."

Harper glanced down at the book in her hand and adjusted

her seat in the grass. "Are you asking whether I want to marry or to teach?"

"I suppose I am."

Harper opened her mouth but shut it without a word. Of course, looking back at the weddings she's witnessed on the wagon train—Cora's and Lark's—she couldn't deny there had been a hint of longing from watching the two women find their happiness. Their joyous celebrations filled Harper's heart with joy. They had found everything she had wanted for them, and like them, she, too, had yearned for the companionship and love that came with marriage. Not to mention the joy that came with children and having a family of her own. Seeing as how she never knew her parents, it would be nice to give a child—or however many God blessed her with—the chance she never had.

But she also couldn't deny that she also wondered if her own path would lead her down the aisle, especially when all she saw in her future was a humble schoolhouse nestled amidst towering trees, with eager young faces eagerly absorbing the lessons she would impart. The vast open spaces of Oregon would become the canvas for her classroom, and the thought brought a smile to her face and filled her heart with warmth.

It was a dream and yet uncertainty, and it gnawed at her, leaving a bittersweet taste in her mouth.

"However," Winona continued as though troubled with Harper's hesitation. "I also suppose you can have both. Should that be your decision."

"That is true. Teachers can marry and have families. They do it all the time." Harper chuckled, nudging the headmistress's arm with her shoulder.

Winona chuckled too. "Yes, it's just the orphanage headmistresses that grow into old spinsters."

"You are far from an old spinster, Winona. And you never know what is waiting for you in Oregon. You might find yourself a fine gentleman who falls head over heels in love from the moment he sees you."

"Highly unlikely, but I do appreciate the kind words."

The two women sat momentarily, looking at the sky as the sun continued rising over the horizon. While Harper didn't know what Winona's thoughts were settled on, she thought of what Oregon would be like. Of course, she knew little about the country. Did it have mountains and valleys? Or was it nothing but vast prairies like they'd seen in Nebraska and Wyoming? Was it green? Was it warm? Was it cold?

Of course, there was a beauty in the unknown, but there was also an anxious unrest that had found its way into her mind, and she both loved and hated the questions that she couldn't answer.

"Well, I suppose we should get to work. Will you help me fetch us some water from the river?" Winona pointed toward the buckets she'd set down, then rose to her feet, brushing any bits of dirt or grass from her skirt. "I have something I wish to discuss with you."

"What is it?"

"You'll see."

***

Harper stood where the sandy edge of the river met the Wyoming prairie with her gaze fixed upon the towering presence of Independence Rock. It stood as a monolith of strength and endurance, an ancient sentinel that had weathered the storms of time. Its rugged exterior, carved by centuries of wind and rain, bore witness to the passage of countless seasons, each etching its story upon the rock's stony face.

She had read once in a news article about how Independence Rock rose defiantly from the earth, reaching toward the heavens with a stoic determination. Its massive form commanded attention, casting a profound shadow across the vast expanse of the prairie. But reading those words and now seeing the rock's sheer magnitude wasn't like anything she had imagined.

Staring at the rock in the distance, her eyes traced the intricate patterns etched into the rock's surface. It was as though the years had given birth to a tapestry of texture and color, with jagged crevices and smooth curves converging in a harmonious dance. The warm hues of orange and gold adorned the rock, and its rugged countenance softened by the gentle touch of sunlight.

Amidst its ancient facade, the rock seemed to hold secrets untold. Names and dates, carved by those who had journeyed westward, adorned its surface like an ardent declaration of their existence, and Harper couldn't help but think that these simple inscriptions represented the dreams and aspirations of pioneers who had traversed the arduous trails of the frontier, leaving behind a tangible mark that they had not only existed but had been this in this very spot she now stood.

Inhaling a deep breath, Harper's gaze swept across the unfurled panorama of the Wyoming prairie. She drank in the splendor of the untamed wilderness that stretched as far as the eye could see. Like a patchwork quilt, the golden hues peeked through the tall grass that swayed gently under the caress of the wind, and its undulating waves whispered stories of the untamed beauty.

She looked around at the different wildflowers growing along the riverbank. They seemed to know the best place to grow where they could drink their fill, unlike the blooms that grew around the camp. They painted the canvas of the land with their vibrant blooms, and the splashes of color popped amidst a sea of green grass.

The Wyoming prairie seemed boundless, a testament to the unyielding spirit of the West. Its vastness stirred something deep within Harper's soul, evoking a sense of humility and wonder. It was a landscape that commanded respect, offering solace to those who sought its embrace.

She felt as though she stood at the intersection of history and natural splendor, where the enduring strength of the rock mirrored the resilience of those who had journeyed before her with untamed dreams. In this captivating tableau, Harper couldn't help but feel an overwhelming sense of gratitude for the opportunity to witness the spirit of the West, the spirit of exploration, and the spirit of boundless possibility.

"So, what is it you wanted to talk about?" Harper asked Winona as she knelt by the water and dunked the bucket into the river, watching it fill before she pulled it out and set it in the sand.

"I spoke to Mrs. Reed and Mrs. Stonemill this morning. It seems they are having trouble with educating the children. It seems all of the parents are. They were wondering if you wanted to help with the problem."

"Help how? Do they want me to teach the children?" Harper's excitement fluttered. She hadn't known what Winona was going to say, but of all the things that it could have been, this was the best one.

"Of course they do. I told them I would ask you, so I'm wondering what you think about the idea?"

"I think I would love it."

"I was hoping you would say that."

WAGON TRAIN WOMEN

Five women headed out West to make new lives on the Frontier find hope and love in the arms of five men. Their adventures may be different, but their bond is the same as they embark on the journey together in the same wagon train.

CHECK OUT THE SERIES ON AMAZON!

Turn the page for a sneak peek at book one, Her Wagon Train Husband.

ONE

ABBY

*E*veryone loves adventure.
   Well, almost everyone.
Abby had to correct herself on that point. Her parents didn't like adventure much. Neither did her three older sisters. They liked being home. They liked being in a place they knew. They didn't enjoy the thrill of the unknown or the sense that the world could open up right under their feet.

Of course, that wasn't an appealing thought. For surely that would mean death. And Abby didn't like the idea of that. She just liked the adventure.

Yeah, she thought to herself. I don't like that.

Abby heaved a deep sigh as she walked along the path around the lake. It was a favorite pastime for her and one she enjoyed nearly every day. Well, every day that her parents and sister's stayed in their country home. When they were in the city . . . well, that was another story. She would often sneak out of the house and head to the park. Even if she had to be careful about being seen, she would still try to get in a little walk in the trees and sunshine. Wasn't that what Spring and Summer were for? Perhaps even Autumn? Winter surely not, although she couldn't complain too much about those months. For she loved the snow too and would enjoy it until her fingers and nose turned red, and her skin hurt.

Something about nature called to her like a mother calls to a child when they want them to come home or to the table to sit down and share a meal. She loved everything about it. The smell of the air, the sound of the birds, and the leaves rustling in the breeze. The feel of the sunshine upon her skin and how it felt as though her body tried to soak it all in like a rag soaks up water.

The outdoors made her feel alive.

Much like the sense of adventure did.

And the two, she thought, went hand in hand.

"Aammeelliiaa!" She heard a woman's voice call out in the distance. Her name was long and drawn out and sounded as though the woman—her mother—calling had her hands up against the sides of her mouth.

Her heart thumped. She couldn't be caught coming from the direction of the lake, and yet, there would be no chance to sneak around to the other side of the stables without being seen. Her mother called for her several more times, and as she tried to round the stables, appearing as though she came from a different direction, she heard her mother's foot stomp on the front porch.

"Abby Lynn Jacobson! And just where have you been?" Her mother raised her hand as if to stop her from answering. "Don't even tell me you were walking around that lake all by yourself."

"All right." Abby squared her shoulders. "I don't tell you that."

Her mother's eyes narrowed, and she pointed her finger in Abby's face. "You listen to me, young lady; you will not go flittering off again. Do you understand me? You have far too many responsibilities in this house to do anything other than what you're supposed to be doing."

"But sewing and cooking and cleaning are just so boring. I want to be outside."

"Outside is no place for a woman unless they are out there to hang laundry on the line or gardening. Both of which you need to be doing too." Her mother continued to wave her hands around the outside of the house, pointing toward the laundry line and the fenced garden around the back of the house. Clothes already hung on the line, and they moved in the breeze. "Your sisters certainly don't spend any time fooling around outside."

"That's because my sisters are married and have husbands to look after."

"And you will have one too. Sooner than later, now that your father has made it official."

"What do you mean?" Abby jerked her head, and her brow furrowed.

"Mr. Herbert Miller is on his way over to the house this afternoon."

"Why?" Although she asked, she wasn't sure she wanted the answer, nor did she believe she would like it.

Her mother shook her head and rolled her eyes. "To finalize the agreement and plans to marry you and take care of you, of course."

Abby sucked in a breath and spit went down the wrong pipe. She choked and sputtered, coughing several times while she gasped. "I . . . I . . ." She coughed a few more times and held out her hand until she regained composure. "I don't want to marry him."

"That's not for you to decide. He comes from a well-to-do family and intends to provide a good life for you. Not to mention we could use the money." Her mother clasped her hands together and fidgeted with her fingers as she glanced around the home. It was still in good shape for its age, but even

Abby had seen some of the repairs it needed, and she knew her parents couldn't afford it. "I dare say he's the richest young man out of all your sister's husbands. You will have a better life than any of them."

"And you think I care about that?"

"You should. It's well known around St. Louis that the Millers have the means. There are mothers and fathers all over the city who would love to have him for a son-in-law. You're going to have quite the life, young lady."

"But is it quite the life if it's a life I don't want?"

"How can you not want it? A husband. A nice home. Children. It's all you've wanted."

"No, it's all you've wanted. And it's all my sisters have wanted."

"Oh, spare me talk of your dreams of adventure." She rolled her eyes again and wiggled her finger at her daughter. "There is plenty of adventure in being married and having children. Trust me."

"That's not the kind of adventure I want, Mother."

"It doesn't matter what you want, Abby. Your purpose in life and in this family is to marry and have children. If you're lucky, which it looks like you are, you will marry a nice man with means. You should be happy. You could have ended up like Mirabel Pickens." Mother brushed her fingers across her forehead. "Lord only knows what her parents were thinking marrying her off to that horrible Mr. Stansbury on the edge of town. He's at least twice her age and hasn't two pennies to rub together. Of course, he acts like he does, but honestly, I think the Pickens family gives them money." Mother fanned her face with her hand. "Now, go upstairs and change your dress. Fix your hair too. He'll be here within the hour."

Before Abby could protest any further, her mother spun on her heel and marched back across the porch and into the back door of the kitchen. Abby stood on the porch. Part of her was too stunned for words, yet the other part wasn't shocked at all. She always knew this day was coming. It just had come a little sooner than she thought it would, and although she had thought of a few excuses or reasons she could give to put it off, with Herbert on his way to the house, she didn't know if any of them would work.

Scratch that.

She knew none of them would work.

Her parents had their eyes set on the young Mr. Miller for a while, and there wasn't any reasoning they would listen to that would change their minds.

It wasn't that Herbert—or Hewy as he once told her she could call him—was a dreadful young man. He wasn't exactly what she would call the type of man she would hope to marry, but he was nice. He was taller than most men his age and skinner, and he wore thick glasses that always seemed to slip down his nose as he talked. He was constantly pushing them back up, and there were times Abby wondered if he ever would buy a pair that fit better or if he enjoyed the fact they were a size too big. Like had it become a habit for him and one he liked.

She remembered how distracting it had been at the Christmas dance last December that her parent's friends hosted at their house. Every few steps, he would take his hand off her waist to push them back up his nose, and he would even miss a step here and there, throwing them both off balance because he had to lead. He'd even stepped on her foot once or twice.

Her toe throbbed for days after that party.

No. She simply could not marry him. She just couldn't.

If her mother wouldn't see reason, perhaps her pa would.

She marched across the porch and into the house, making her way toward his office and knocking on the door.

"Come in," her pa said from the other side, and as she

opened it and moved into the room, he glanced up from his desk and smiled. "Good afternoon, Abby."

"Well, it's an afternoon, but I'm not sure it's a good one."

He cocked one eyebrow and threw the pencil in his hand down onto a stack of papers on the desk. "What has your mother done now?"

"She's informed me that Mr. Herbert Miller is on his way to the house to finalize an agreement for my hand in marriage." She paused for a moment but then continued before her father could say a word. "Father, I know you aren't going to accept it. Right?"

"And what makes you say that?" He glanced down at the papers on his desk as he blew out a breath.

She knew where this conversation was headed. She'd seen this reaction in him she didn't know how many times in her life. When faced with a question that Pa didn't want to answer, he used work as his excuse to ask whoever was asking him what he didn't want to face to leave. She wasn't about to let him do it today.

"I don't care what you have on that desk that is so important, Pa, but quite frankly, I don't care. This is important. This is my future. I don't want to marry Herbert Miller. I don't love him. You've got to put a stop to this."

He reached up and rubbed his fingers into his temples. "What is it that you want me to say, Abby? I don't have time for this."

"I want you to say no and tell him that I'm not ready to marry and that you don't give him your blessing."

"You know I can't say that, young lady."

"For heaven's sakes, why not?"

"Because we've already agreed, and he's already paid off our debts."

"He's done what?" She didn't mean to shout, but she did anyway, and the look on her father's face as the loudness in her tone blared in his ears told her she should have given a second thought before letting her volume raise.

"Don't take that tone with me, young lady."

"I'm sorry, Pa. I didn't mean to. It's just that . . . I don't want to marry Herbert Miller."

"And I don't understand why you don't. He comes from a good family—"

"And he wants to provide me with a good life. I know." She threw her hands up in the air and paced in front of her father's desk. "Mother already told me all those things. But they don't matter. It doesn't matter how good his family is or what he wants to provide for me. I don't want to be like my sisters. You know this. You've always known this."

"Don't tell me you still have all those silly notions of adventure stuck in your head."

"They aren't silly."

"But they are!" He slapped his hand down on his desk. The force was so great that it rattled the oil lamp sitting on the edge, and the flame flickered. Abby flinched, and she stared at her pa, blinking.

Of course, she'd seen her father angry a time or two growing up. She didn't think there was a child alive who didn't see their parents in a fit at least once. It was what adults did.

But while she knew he could get that angry, she didn't expect to see it. At least not today. Not over this.

He fetched an envelope, opened it, and yanked out the money tucked inside. He threw it down on the table. "Do you see this? This is what will save this family. You are what will save this family. Abby, it's time you grow up and stop wasting your time and thoughts on silly things. You're not a child anymore. You're a woman. It's time for you to marry and take care of a husband and children. I know you have never talked about wanting those things, but I thought perhaps the older you became . . ."

"Well, you thought wrong." She folded her arms across her chest.

"Perhaps I did. But that doesn't change the fact that we will make the wedding plans when this young man comes over this afternoon."

"Pa, please, no. Don't make me do this."

He held up his hands. "I'm sorry, Abby, but I've already made my decision, and the deal is done. It's what I had to do to save this house and my family. And it was the best thing I could have done for you." He moved to the office door, opening it before he paused in the frame. "Now, if you'll excuse me, I must see to the rest of my work before this young man arrives."

"Pa?"

"Abby, this conversation is finished."

Tears welled in her eyes, and although she tried to blink them away, she couldn't, and they soon found themselves spilling over and streaming down her cheeks. She shook her head as she watched him leave the office. While she knew there had been a chance he wouldn't listen to her, she hoped he might.

And now that hope was gone, leaving her with only a sense of desperation.

What could she do? She couldn't marry Herbert. She just couldn't. She would rather run away than marry him.

Run away.

That was what she would do.

That was the answer.

If she wanted adventure when no one would give it to her, well then, she would simply take it for herself.

All she needed was to pack some clothes and get her hands on some money.

Money.

She glanced over her shoulder toward the pile of cash Pa had yanked out of the envelope. She didn't know how much was there, but it looked enough. Or she should say it looked like enough to get her where she wanted to go. It was hers after all, wasn't it? If she was the one sold like a farm animal?

She moved over to the desk, staring down at the paper bills.

She didn't have to take it all. She could leave some of it for her parents.

Never mind, she thought. *I'm taking every last dollar.*

TWO

WILLIAM

"Do you have room for my horse?"

William's eyes fluttered with the booming voice that filtered into the barn from the stalls and walkway below. He rolled over, and several stalks of hay poked his back through his shirt. He hated sleeping in the hayloft of a barn, but it was safer than sleeping in a stall. Not only could a horse step on him, or worse, lay down on him in a stall, but there was a better chance he would get caught if he was down there instead of up in the hayloft.

And he couldn't get caught.

Not unless he wanted to go to jail.

Which he didn't.

"Yeah. Just take the last stall on the left, Mr. Russell. Are you boarding for the day?" another voice asked.

"I'll be back for him around dawn. That's when we leave to take another trip to Oregon. I gots me a pocket full of money, and I want to have fun spending it."

William's ears perked up with the word money, and he rolled over again, scooting on his stomach toward the edge of the loft so he could look down upon the man. He couldn't glimpse the man's face looking down on the top of his hat, but the man was dressed in all black from his hat to his chaps. He watched as the man led his buckskin horse down the walkway into the stall and untacked it before throwing the saddle on the rack and hooking the bridle on the horn. He fed and watered the animal, then strode back toward the door. The rowels of his spurs clanked and rattled with each of his steps.

William knew he needed to get out of the barn before the stable master found him. He didn't know the price he would have to pay if caught sleeping in the hayloft, but he wasn't about to find out. He rolled up onto his knees, folding his blanket before shoving it in his bag and brushing the last crumbs of the stale loaf of bread he had for dinner, so they scattered in the hay.

Looking over the edge of the loft, he glanced around, and after making sure no one would see him, he scaled down the ladder, jumping off the last rung before he slung his bag over his shoulder and darted out the back door of the barn.

~

William hadn't ever been to Independence, Missouri before. He'd only heard about it in his brother's stories. They used to talk about coming here as young boys when they dreamed. It was known as the Queen City of the Trails. The starting point where those seeking to travel out west to the frontier started their journey. He hadn't known what to expect from this strange little city, but such didn't matter. All that did was that somehow, he found his way out of it.

And preferably by wagon on a wagon train headed to Oregon or California.

He wasn't picky about where he would go. He just needed to

get as far away from Missouri as possible and by any means he could.

Even if he had to work for it.

He trotted down the different alleyways between the buildings, staying off the main streets as he veered through town. He rounded the corner onto another street, and as he did, he came face to face with a small café. Scents of eggs, bacon, sausage, and potatoes wafted in the air, and his stomach growled as though to tell him it wanted everything the nose could smell. His mouth watered too, and he closed his eyes, imagining how it all tasted—which he was sure was delicious.

He hadn't eaten anything since finding that loaf of old bread in the garbage outside of the bakery yesterday morning, and while he had planned to go back there to check for more, the thought of stale, butterless bread was no match for the smell of a hot breakfast.

Opening his eyes, he glanced down at the ground. He didn't want more stale bread any more than he wanted to dig out his own eyes, but of course, there was one big problem. How to get it? Getting the bread was easy, but with empty pockets and not a nickel to his name, the hot breakfast was nothing short of impossible.

He heaved a deep sigh and hunched his shoulders as he kicked at a rock and watched it roll several inches. Admitting defeat was never easy, and this morning with a grumbling stomach was no exception.

Still, facts were facts. He didn't have the money, so bread it was.

He continued down the street, barely looking up as he passed the café. He didn't want to see the food any more than he wanted to smell it, but as he passed, he glanced out of the corner of his eye. A young couple was sitting at a table outside, chatting to one another. Distracted with their conversation, they didn't even look at William as he passed. Hesitation spurred through him, and he slowed down, watching as the man scooted his chair toward the woman, and they huddled their faces close to one another.

"And so, I told him, Mr. Dexter, I just can't marry your daughter because I'm in love with someone else," the man said.

"Oh, and just who might that be?" the woman asked.

The man scooted his chair even closer and grabbed her hands. "Why, you, my darling." While the woman ducked her chin, her face turned a bright shade of red, and she removed her handkerchief from her handbag, brushing her other hand along her chest. William wanted to retch at the sight of their love and affection for one another, but with an empty stomach, nothing would have come up. Not to mention, he would have drawn unwanted attention from what he was about to do.

He just needed to wait for the perfect moment...

Just as he had hoped, the man, so overcome with love, shoved his plate aside and out of his way. William lunged over the small fence separating the dining area from the sidewalk and grabbed the plate. The woman screamed, but as the man spun in his chair, William took off down the street with the plate tucked tight into his body so none of the food would spill.

William continued down the street and around another building, hiding behind several wooden crates stacked against the brick wall. He pressed his back against the bricks and glanced down both directions of the alleyway before sliding down to the ground and tucking his legs up until he was blocked from sight.

His lungs heaved, and he closed his eyes. "Lord. Please forgive me for stealing this food. I know it's wrong, and I have sinned. I hate to eat it, but . . . I'm starving. I pray for my forgiveness. In Jesus' name. Amen."

Although the first bite tasted like a little bit of heaven, the guilt gave it an unpleasant aftertaste. It was one he didn't like, but he also knew that he didn't know when he would see food again without stealing. He wanted to curse himself just as much as he wanted to curse his brother for putting him into this mess. And yet, he also knew that doing either of those wouldn't make the situation better.

Nothing would make it better.

Well, clearing his name would.

But knowing the solution and putting it into play were two different things. Pinkertons weren't about hearing reason. They just saw the words as excuses. The guilty are always trying to get out of punishment for their crimes, they would say, and no matter what he told them, they would only say it to him.

They wouldn't believe him.

Nor would they even give him the chance to explain.

He shoveled the last few bites of eggs into his mouth, both wanting to chew them slowly to savor them and also gobble them down so he could flee before anyone caught him. Once he had licked it clean, he tossed the plate aside, and another hint of guilt prickled in his chest as the bone white china smacked against the dirt with a thud sound. He wanted to return the plate to the café, and yet he knew that it would be foolish to do so.

Perhaps I can leave it outside the door tonight after dark, he thought. Do at least one good thing today, even if it's not much of one.

It would be the right thing to do.

He could almost hear his mama talking to him from Heaven above, telling him what he needed to do. Or course, that was nothing new. He listened to her daily, always on his case about one thing or another he did. Lord, she would roll over in her grave if she saw him now. He was glad she passed on so she wouldn't have to see the utter failure he'd become. As much as he hated to think that, he did, and it was just another thing to hate his brother for.

He heaved a deep sigh and slipped his hand into his pants pocket, pulling out a folded piece of paper. It was yellower than it had been months ago, and the edges were tearing from all the time spent in his pocket, and all the times he pulled it out, looked at it, and stuck it back in. It wasn't that looking at it gave him hope or comfort. It was just the opposite, actually. The paper only brought him fear, pain, and anger, and although he wanted to throw it away every second of every day, he also wanted to keep it. He didn't know why.

Perhaps it was the reminder he needed.

Or perhaps he was nothing but an utter fool.

He didn't know which.

But as he opened it and looked down upon the words 'WANTED' and a drawn picture of his face with his name below written in black ink, all the feelings came flooding back.

He was a wanted man.

And it was all his brother's fault.

ORDER OR READ FOR FREE WITH KINDLE UNLIMITED

BRIDES OF LONE HOLLOW

Five men looking for love...

Five women with different ideas...

One small town where they all will either live happily ever after or leave with shattered dreams.

Order the series today or Read for FREE with Kindle Unlimited

Turn the page for a sneak peek at book one, Her Mail Order Mix-Up.

ONE

CULLEN

"God never gives you what He can't carry you through."

Pastor Duncan's words repeated in Cullen McCray's mind as he glanced down at his niece. All of just nine years old, the little girl sat beside him in the wagon as they drove into town. Her little body bumped into his every time a wheel rolled over a rock, and her white-blonde hair blew in the gentle breeze. She was the purest example of what the pastor was talking about. Or at least that was what the pastor had told him when he brought her to Cullen's cabin that day, scared and sad. Her entire world was torn apart by her father's sudden death and him, her uncle, her only chance.

She glanced back at him. Her eyes---his brother's eyes---stared at him. She looked more like Clint every day, and he wondered if she would grow up to have Clint's mannerisms. Would she act like him? Talk like him? Would she think like him? While he wanted her to, a part of him didn't. He wasn't sure he wanted another Clint in his life.

"What do we need from town today, Uncle Cullen?" Sadie asked.

He rolled the piece of straw from one side of his lips to the other, chewing a little more on the sweet taste of the dried stem. "Just the usual, Sadie. Did you need something else this time?"

She shrugged. "I was thinking of making a pie when we got back to the ranch."

Pie.

He hadn't thought of pie in months, hadn't thought about much of the things his late wife used to bake, actually. Because thinking of them would have reminded him of her and how she wasn't around to bake them anymore. He ate chili and stew and steak and potatoes and eggs and bacon, which was the sum of his diet. Perhaps he would have some bread or biscuits on those cold winter nights when he needed something to stick to the sides of his gut and keep him warm, but other than that, he didn't branch out. He didn't want to. He didn't want the reminder.

Of course, he knew that needed to change now that Sadie was in his life. He had to care for her, and a little growing girl needed more nourishment than what he'd been putting into his body. She needed a garden with lots of vegetables and an orchard with fruit trees. She needed bread. She needed cakes and cookies and, well, pie. All the things his late wife would spend her days making for him. He could still smell all the scents in the house. But back to the point. Sadie needed more, and she also needed to cook and bake—or at least learn to do those things along with how to sew, read, and do arithmetic.

"Do you know how to bake a pie?" he asked the girl.

"I do. Well, sort of. It was one thing Nanny Noreen taught me before . . ." The little girl's voice trailed off. She didn't want to say before the accident. She never did. She always stopped herself when she found the words trying to come out of her lips.

Not that he blamed her. He never wished to speak of it, either. His brother and his sister-in-law were now up in Heaven with his wife, leaving Sadie and him down here on earth to pick up the pieces as best as they could.

"What kind of pie did you want to make?" he asked; a slight hope rose in his chest that the girl would say peach or apple. Those were always his favorite.

"I don't know. I guess whatever fruit I can find in town."

Find in town.

Guilt prickled in his chest. She shouldn't have to find fruit in town. She should be able to go out and pick it off her tree. It was just another thing he mentally put on his list of things to do for her—plant some trees.

"Well, I suppose we can look to see what Mr. Dawson has. If you find something that works, we can get it. Did you need anything else for a pie?"

"I don't know. I suppose if I may, I'll look around?"

"Yeah. You can do that."

She glanced at him again and smiled before leaning her head on his arm.

His heart gave another little tug at his guilt. For so many months after the accident and after Pastor Duncan brought her up to his cabin, he hadn't wanted her to stay. Not quite a burden, but almost there. He had packed her bags, he didn't know how many times, fully intent on taking her down to the orphanage where he thought she belonged. She needed a chance at a family with a ma and pa. She didn't need a gruff lone wolf like him. Not to mention, he had wished to live his life alone in his cabin. The cattle ranch. The family. Those were all things Clint, his brother, wanted. He didn't. Or at least he didn't until . . .

He shook his head, ridding himself of the thoughts of his late wife.

He couldn't think of her.

Not now.

Not today.

Never again.

He tapped the reins on the horses' backs, then whistled at them to pick up the pace into a trot. He needed the distraction of town to ease his mind.

MAGGIE

"Love always, Clint." Maggie once again read the ending words of Clint's last letter as the stagecoach rolled down the lane. Her heart thumped, and she bit her lip as she leaned back in the seat and rested her head back.

She didn't want to think about the life she left to travel hundreds of miles across the United States so she could marry a man she didn't know. Or how she fled her parents' house in the middle of the night with her mother telling her to leave while her father slept. She only wanted to think about the life she was about to start as Mrs. Clint McCray. It didn't matter that they hadn't actually met before and had only corresponded with letters. Nor did it matter that she wasn't exactly in love with him . . . yet. It only mattered that in those letters, he promised her a life far away from her parents and the life they had planned for her. One where Daddy would shove her into a loveless marriage with either Benjamin Stone or Matthew Cooper—two sons of business acquaintances he'd known for years. She knew both men well, too. Benjamin was nothing but a bore, and Matthew . . . well, let her just say she didn't care for the way he treated women. Not to mention, his reputation in town left little to be desired, and she doubted the perpetual bachelor would even want to marry. He had more fun pursuing other tastes.

While she knew her daddy didn't think they were the best choices, he also wasn't about to have a spinster for a daughter, and she knew her time was fast ticking away. As did her mama. Which was why, when Clint's letter arrived with the plan for her to leave, they packed her a suitcase and bought her a ticket out west. Out to Lone Hollow, Montana.

"Are you headed to Lone Hollow?" the woman sitting across from her asked. Slightly older than Maggie, her hair was styled in a tight bun at the base of her neck, and she looked through a pair of spectacles resting on her long, thin nose.

"Yes, I am. My soon-to-be husband lives there and is waiting for me."

The woman smiled and ducked her chin slightly. "Best wishes to you both."

"Thank you. I'm Maggie, by the way. Maggie Colton."

The woman nodded. "Amelia Hawthorn. It's a pleasure to meet you."

"You, too." Maggie shifted her gaze from the woman to the window of the stagecoach. Nothing but mountains and forests and wilderness, Montana had been nothing like she'd ever seen before. So pretty. So peaceful. Like God's perfect place and glory was here in this state. "Where are you headed?" she asked, turning her attention to the woman.

"Brook Creek. It's about forty miles west of Lone Hollow."

"So, you still have a bit to go in your travels."

"Unfortunately. But I figure I've been this far. As long as I get to my post, I don't mind the distance."

"Post?"

"I'm a schoolteacher, and I received my post orders for the small town. I had asked for Lone Hollow, seeing as how it's a milling town, but was told it was filled . . . at least for now."

"A milling town? Does that make it a more appealing post?"

"A little. Lone Hollow has one of the few sawmills around,

and having a sawmill means more amenities than Brook Creek, like a hotel and café. There is more of a population in Lone Hollow than in Brook Creek, too, which means there are more families and children. They told me they would tell me if the teacher in Lone Hollow leaves, and if he does, then I will move again as I'm not sure I want to stay in Brook Creek."

The name made Maggie giggle. "It's funny that the town is named for two synonyms for a river."

"Don't get me started on that." The woman rolled her eyes and exhaled a deep sigh as she slid her fingers behind her ears, tucking any loose strands of her blonde bun behind her ears. The feathers on her maroon hat fluttered with her movement, and they matched her maroon dress. "Of course, all I care about are the children. I hope they are nice and are ready to learn."

"I'm sure they are, and you will do fine." Maggie bit her lip again at the thoughts in her head. She dropped her gaze to her hands, fidgeting with her fingers. "My husband-to-be has a daughter. She is nine years old. His first wife died of Scarlet Fever several years ago when she was just a baby. I feel awful that she was never able to meet her mother."

"Such a shame she lost her mama."

"Yes, it is. I just hope I can bond with her. I don't wish to replace her mother, but I hope to be someone she can accept and love."

"I'm sure she will. It might take some time, but you will do just fine."

Maggie glanced at the woman and smiled as she nodded. She didn't know if she could talk anymore about the young girl or her concerns, for the notions brought more butterflies to her stomach than the thoughts of meeting Clint. She wanted to do right by the young girl and wanted to be someone the girl could trust, look up to, and perhaps love after time had passed. She knew how wonderful it was to grow up with a mother, and she wanted that for Sadie.

The stagecoach slowed, and with the change of pace, Maggie glanced out the window again. While the mountains and forests were still in her view, a few houses speckled what little she could see, and as more and more passed by, the stagecoach slowed as it finally entered the town of Lone Hollow.

TWO

CULLEN

Cullen halted the horses in front of the general store, and as Sadie climbed from the wagon and trotted inside, he jumped down himself and tied the reins to the tie post. The morning sun shone down on the back of his neck, causing a thin layer of sweat that he wiped away after yanking the handkerchief from his back pocket. He made a mental note of the things he needed—sugar, flour, more seeds for their new garden, and some much-needed equipment to help him with the tasks. How Clint had tended to the old garden they had at the ranch in past years with the broken and rusted tools in the barn, he didn't know.

He also didn't want to forget he needed nails for the lumber he picked up from the sawmill the other day. The old barn had a wall that needed fixing before winter set in, or else he didn't think it would withstand another few months of the wind, ice, and snow.

Actually, the whole thing needed fixing—or to be replaced—but he wanted to at least take it one wall at a time.

"Good morning, Mr. McCray." Mr. Dawson smiled as Cullen

entered the store. His voice boomed over the bell that chimed as the door opened the closed.

"Morning."

"I saw Sadie run past a few minutes ago. She darted over in the corner as though she was determined to find something." The owner slightly chuckled as he adjusted his glasses up his nose.

"She's fixing to make a pie this afternoon."

"Oh? A pie. Sounds delicious. I have some nice apples that Mr. Smith brought in yesterday from his orchard. I tried one myself, and they are bright red on the outside and juicy on the inside. They should make some lovely pies."

"Well, then I suppose I see an apple pie in my future for dinner, then."

The two men chuckled at Cullen's joke as Cullen leaned against the counter.

"So, what can I do for you today?" Mr. Dawson asked.

"Just the usual. Plus, I need a new rake, hoe, and shovel. I'm going to expand the garden at the ranch this spring. Let Sadie have fun growing what we will eat in the winter."

"Sounds like she'll enjoy that."

Cullen ducked his chin for a moment, lowering his voice. "I sure hope so."

Mr. Dawson laid his hand on Cullen's shoulder. "Mrs. Dawson and I were talking about what happened to your brother and how you've taken the girl in and cared for her. You're doing a mighty fine thing, Mr. McCray, and a mighty fine job, too. The whole town thinks so. You shouldn't doubt yourself."

Cullen nodded. "Thank you. I'm trying. Sometimes I do not know why God gave a guy like me a girl to raise."

"Because He knows what He's doing."

The door opened, and the bell above it chimed again. Cullen glanced over, meeting Pastor Duncan's gaze as he strolled in.

The pastor nodded and tipped his hat to the two men before taking it off and tossing it on the counter.

"Morning, gentlemen," he said.

"Morning, Pastor." While Mr. Dawson returned the salutation, Cullen only nodded. An air of being uncomfortable squared in his chest. He hadn't seen the pastor in a while, and the last time he did was when the pastor brought Sadie up to his cabin with the news . . . and well, he hadn't been pleasant to the old man. In fact, he'd been downright rude, and while at the time he thought he was justified, there were times he felt he'd overreacted.

Pastor Duncan nodded back to the store owner and yanked a slip of paper from his pocket. "Mr. Dawson, I have some special requests I need to make this morning, and I'm hoping you don't have to order any of them."

"Sure thing." Mr. Dawson held out his hand. "Give me the order. I'll see what I can do after I get Mr. McCray loaded."

"Oh, there's no need for that. Just bring what you have for me out here. I'll load it myself," Cullen said, hoping the gesture would make up—even if it were just a little—for the past.

"Are you sure?"

"Yes, I'm sure. See to the Pastor's order. I'm in no hurry."

As Mr. Dawson vanished in the store's backroom, Pastor Duncan leaned against the counter. He glanced at Cullen a few times before clearing his throat. "Did you bring Miss Sadie with you?"

"She's over there, gathering things to make a pie this afternoon."

"A pie?" The pastor's eyebrows raised as he smiled. "Sounds like you will have a splendid dinner this evening."

"If she doesn't burn the house down." Cullen chuckled to himself a bit.

"It also sounds like she's doing all right. After . . . everything."

"She seems to be. She has her moments as I would expect anyone to have, having been through what she's been through."

"And how are you handling everything?"

"All right, too, I suppose." He paused for a moment, clearing his throat. "Listen, Pastor, about the last time we spoke—"

"There's nothing to say about that."

"But there is. I wasn't . . . I was rude to you, and I shouldn't have been. I can't imagine it was easy for you, bringing Sadie to my cabin with the news."

"It wasn't that bad. I figure since it was His plan, I might as well help Him orchestrate it." The pastor smiled. "We haven't seen you around church lately. I was hoping you would start coming again now that you have Sadie."

A flicker of guilt prickled in Cullen's chest. He knew how wrong it was to skip church every week. But it had been the one thing he and his wife shared, had been their favorite time together, and since her death, he hadn't been able to even think about setting foot inside that place. Every inch screamed her. Every wooden pew. Every window. The door. The pulpit. Even the floor that she'd walked down dressed in a white dress to become his wife.

Now she lay in the ground in the small graveyard next to it.

That was another reason he hadn't been back. He hadn't visited her grave since the funeral.

"I'll think about next Sunday, and I'll ask Sadie if she wants to go," he lied.

Pastor Duncan's eyes narrowed for a moment before they softened. "Children rarely know what's best for them, and it's up to their parents to tell them what they need to learn and do."

"Yeah, well, I'm not her parent."

"You are. It's just a different kind of parent."

Cullen opened his mouth to argue again but stopped himself as the little girl bounded around one of the shelves. A broad grin etched across her face as she held an armful of bright red apples.

"Uncle Cullen! Uncle Cullen! Mr. Dawson has apples. Lots of red and juicy-looking apples. I think I'll try to make an apple pie, maybe even two pies. What do you think?"

"I think it sounds delicious, Sadie."

Her smile widened even more, and she handed him every one, she carried.

"Hello, Pastor Duncan," she said, noticing him standing there.

"Good morning, Sadie. How are you this fine morning?"

"Good." A memory seemed to flicker in her mind, and her face twisted a little. Her smile faded. While Cullen wasn't sure of the thoughts suddenly weighing on her mind, he could guess that it had to do with the fact that the last time she'd seen the pastor was when he brought her to Cullen's cabin to let Cullen know, not only of his brother's death but that Sadie was now in his custody. He didn't want to imagine what that time had been like for her. Having lived through both her parents' deaths, she was now an orphan and coming to live with a man she only knew a little.

As Cullen put the apples on the counter, Mr. Dawson returned from the back with his arms full. "I was able to gather most of what you needed, Pastor Duncan," he said, setting it all down.

"It's a sign from God, then. It's going to be a great day."

Cullen stepped away from the counter as the pastor and store owner finished their transaction. A small part of him hoped the subject of church wouldn't come up again, at least not in front of Sadie, before he had a chance to talk to her. He didn't know if he wanted even to mention it, at least not until he was ready—which he was far from it—and he didn't need the pressure of being roped into it before then.

The pastor said nothing, however, and after paying for his

supplies, he tipped his hat to them, gave Sadie an extra wave and a smile, and left the store without another word.

Cullen breathed a sigh of relief as he laid his hand on Sadie's shoulder and guided her around the counter. "Let's help Mr. Dawson get our supplies from the back and then get them loaded into our wagon."

～

MAGGIE

The stagecoach came to a complete stop in front of the Lone Hollow Hotel, and Maggie climbed out. Her boots touched down on the dirt road, and she lifted her hand to shield her eyes from the sun. It helped a little, but she still had to squint as she glanced from one direction to the other. Clint had said he would wait for her at the hotel, but no one had even approached her as the driver handed over her luggage. Shrugging off the slight air of confusion, she crossed the hotel's porch and sat down on a bench just outside the door. The wood planks showed little kindness to her shoes as the humid moisture in the air stuck to her skin. The sun's heat deepened, weighing on her with a heavy thickness.

Perhaps he got tied up or something and is just running late, she thought.

As the stagecoach's driver finished unloading a few parcels that were obviously en route to people who lived in the town, he climbed back into his seat and cued the horses down the road. Maggie could see Amelia wave just before the carriage vanished around the corner, and she couldn't help but smile when she thought of the small town of Brook Creek.

Who names these towns, anyway, she thought.

People meandered through the streets while Maggie continued to wait on the bench under the overhang, and she glanced around at the hotel to keep her mind busy. It wasn't the worst one she'd ever seen, but it wasn't the best either, looking as though years of weathered seasons had taken a toll on the old wood—the once bright shade of dark red paint had faded into a pale cherry color.

"Top of the mornin' to yeh, Miss," called a voice from the building across the street. She jerked her head around to find a short, plump man tipping his hat to a woman walking toward him. The woman smiled and waved as she passed, and he watched her for a moment before returning to the sweeping he had been doing on the porch in front of a building that looked like a café. The volume of his thick Irish accent overwhelmed the chirping birds in the oak trees above, and he turned his body slightly as a pair of young boys ran past him, one betting the other he could leap up and batter the painted sign while the other could not. However, upon catching the man's glare, they both seemed to realize their theory would go unproven.

More people meandered along the storefront while a man tossed supplies into the back of a wagon while a little girl watched. Her white-blonde curls bounced from not only her movement but the gentle breeze in the air.

Maggie checked her pocket watch. The stagecoach hadn't been early or late, but right on time, and a flicker of concern rested in her stomach. She had gotten the correct date, hadn't she? She reached into her handbag and yanked out the letter, unfolding it as she read it one more time.

"You should arrive on the 10th of April by wagon. I will wait for you." She read the words of Clint's letter in a whisper to herself.

Today was the 10th of April, was it not? She was certain it was.

"Good morning, Miss," a voice said.

She glanced up. Her heart thumped.

"Are you new in town?" The older gentleman said. He tipped his hat before taking it off. "My name is Pastor John Duncan."

She let out a deep breath and stood. "Miss Maggie Colton."

"Sorry for the intrusion. I just saw you sitting here, and it looked as though you were waiting for someone."

"I am. Mr. Clint McCray. I'm his . . . wife-to-be, I suppose you could say. We've been corresponding for several months, and he sent for me so we can be married." She showed him the envelope and piece of paper she was reading as though she thought it would prove her story. Not that she thought the pastor didn't believe her, it just seemed like the thing to do.

He didn't take it, and instead, he jerked his head and blinked as though shocked.

Her stomach twisted. What had she said that seemed wrong? Perhaps she should give a little more detail, hoping to gain some insight into what the pastor was thinking. "He said he would wait for me when I arrived. See? It's all here in this letter. Do you know him?"

"Well, yes, I do . . . but . . ." The pastor glanced over his shoulder, hooking his thumb. He paused for a moment as though watching someone, then turned back to her. "Actually, Mr. McCray is just over there, loading supplies into his wagon."

She had noticed the man earlier. Perhaps he had wanted to get everything loaded before he came for her. "Ah, yes, that man with his daughter. I see. Her name is Sadie, correct?"

"That would be them—Mr. McCray and Sadie McCray." Pastor Duncan moved, stepping aside and motioning her toward the road as if to give her permission to cross it so she could finally be with the one she'd been waiting on. "It was a pleasure meeting you, Miss Colton."

"The pleasure is all mine." She shook his hand again, then bent down, grabbing her suitcases before she looked in both directions and trekked across the road.

Her heart thumped with each step, and as she neared Clint,

she blew out a breath. This was it. This was their moment. The one she could picture in her mind. He would smile. She would smile. They would hug and tell each other how happy they were to meet each other finally. He was more handsome than she had even thought. With broad shoulders and this rough exterior with chocolate hair, a subtle beard, and arms that as they tossed bags of supplies in the wagon, she imagined them wrapped around her. Her excitement fluttered in her chest, and she had to remind herself to walk, not run, to him.

"Mr. McCray?" she called out, and as Clint turned to face her, she dropped her bags and threw her arms out, wrapping them around his neck. Perhaps it wasn't exactly proper of her, but she couldn't help herself, not to mention she didn't care. "I can't believe we are finally meeting."

Clint wiggled from her grasp and backed away from her. His eyes grew wide, and his mouth gaped for a moment. "Who are you?" he asked.

"What do you mean, who am I? I'm Maggie, Maggie Colton. Your soon-to-be wife. You sent for me, and you were supposed to meet me. Remember? It's the 10th of April." Her stomach twisted with each of her words, and with each passing second that the words didn't seem to bring any clarity to him. She still had his letter in her hand, and she outstretched it. "You wrote me, telling me to come so that you and I would be married."

ORDER THE SERIES TODAY OR READ FOR **FREE** WITH KINDLE UNLIMITED

*To my sister
Michelle Renee Horning*

*April 3, 1971 - January 8, 2022
You will be forever missed. I don't know how I'm going to do this thing
called life without you.*

London James is a pen name for Angela Christina Archer. She lives on a ranch with her husband, two daughters, and many farm animals. She was born and raised in Nevada and grew up riding and showing horses. While she doesn't show anymore, she still loves to trail ride.

From a young age, she always wanted to write a novel. However, every time the desire flickered, she shoved the thought from my mind until one morning in 2009, she awoke with the determination to follow her dream.

WWW.AUTHORLONDONJAMES.COM

Join my mailing list for news on releases, discounted sales, and exclusive member-only benefits!

Copyright © 2023

Cover Design by Long Valley Designs

This book is a work of fiction. The names, characters, places, and incidents are the products of the author's imagination or are used fictitiously.

Any resemblance to actual events, business establishments, locales, or persons, living or dead, is entirely coincidental.

All rights reserved.

No part of this publication may be reproduced, stored in retrieval system, or transmitted in any form or by any means (electronic, mechanical, photocopying, recording, or otherwise) without prior written permission of both the copyright owner and the publisher. The only exception is brief quotations in printed reviews.

The scanning, uploading, and distribution of this book via the Internet or via any other means without the permission of the publisher is illegal and punishable by law.

Please purchase only authorized electronic editions and do not participate in or encourage electronic piracy of copyrighted materials.

Your support of the author's rights is appreciated.

Published in the United States of America by:

Long Valley Press
Newcastle, Oklahoma
www.longvalleypress.com
ISBN 978-1-960443-15-1

Scriptures taken from the Holy Bible, New International Version®, NIV®. Copyright © 1973, 1978, 1984, 2011 by Biblica, Inc.™ Used by permission of Zondervan. All rights reserved worldwide. www.zondervan.com The "NIV" and "New International Version" are trademarks registered in the United States Patent and Trademark Office by Biblica, Inc.™

Made in the USA
Middletown, DE
20 September 2023